Pike Place

৶ ৶

A Novel

Marilyn Howard Tschudi

QUARRYSTONE PUBLISHING CO.
NEW YORK

Published by

Quarrystone Publishing Co.

1133 Broadway | Suite 706

New York, NY 10010

info@quarrystonepublishing.com

Printed in the United States of America

Cover Design by Enrico Leoni

Library of Congress Cataloging-in-Publication Data

Tschudi, Marilyn Howard.
Pike Place/by Marilyn Howard Tschudi.— 2nd ed. (pbk.)

ISBN 978-0-6151-4455-9

Pike Place

෯ ෯

Dedicated to
Andrew Boyd Howard

☙ 1 ❧

It had been a while since I rambled across the cobblestone streets of downtown Seattle. I was early, so I took my time and allowed myself to be drawn with the crowd into Pike Place Market. Stall after stall was laden with a Thanksgiving harvest: apples and peaches, asparagus, potatoes, pumpkins, early-winter squash, and – of course – the day's catch. Besides halibut, prawns, and Dungeness crab, I saw at least five types of salmon: Chinook, Sockeye, Coho, Pink, and Chum. That's what I wanted for lunch, the Chum. In just a few minutes, I would be meeting my family at Café Sport, a restaurant that everyone was talking about. It was good to be home.

I was back from New Orleans for the holiday weekend. It was strange to think that people in the south barely knew that this part of the world existed. They had a different perspective of the country down there. Many were still conflicted by the War of Northern Aggression – anyone from the other side of the Mason-Dixon Line was still considered to be a Yankee. Folks in the south didn't know how to label me. I was from the west, but I wasn't from California. I was from the north, but I wasn't a Yankee. To them, Washington was the nation's capital. But to me, Washington could only mean the Pacific Northwest.

I was born in a small town in the southeast corner of Washington. It was a city that was developed by the government during the Second World War. The purpose of moving individuals, mostly engineers, to this arid, obscure place was to develop the nuclear bomb. First there was dirt, and then there was a city, Richland. Neat little houses were built in neat rectangular blocks. Trees were planted and irrigated with great diligence. Churches were built, even a synagogue, and municipal buildings, schools, libraries, and parks soon followed. The plant, out in Hanford, was out of sight of this residential haven, and men would take the bus every morning to get there, and every evening to get back home. It was, in a way, an idyllic childhood. We were white and black and Asian and Hispanic and we were all engineers, or families who belonged to engineers. If there was ever a place to grow up completely color-blind, it was Richland, Washington. Maybe this is just my own recollection of this little town, or maybe it really was as devoid of prejudice as I remember it to be. In any case, I grew up blissfully, without any real sense of need.

I had a friend, a true-blue friend, who I met when I was four and she was two. Her name was Elizabeth Ann Gardiner, and she was the easiest-going child ever born on this earth. I was always full of great ideas as to how we could spend our day, and Lizzie always agreed that my ideas were great. Whether it was making mud pies and selling them to our neighbors, or jumping off of the highest tree limb in my back yard, Lizzie was game. I will never forget the time that I convinced her that it would be fun to climb up on the roof of the junior high school to find Frisbees and tennis balls. Lizzie was a petite little thing and I was always tall for my age. I got up first by way of the big air-conditioning unit in the back of the school. Lizzie had a little difficulty, but I lay on my tummy and reached down for her, grabbing her wrist and heave-ho-ing with all of my might. I got her up there, but not without gouging a little flesh out of her arm. I felt terrible. But I was also scared.

"Please, Lizzie, don't tell your mom how this happened!" She promised that she would never tell, and that it didn't really hurt that much anyway, so we happily danced around on the roof, picking up as many tennis balls as we could stuff into our shirts. We had been sure that we would find untold treasures up on the roof, and we were not disappointed. What an incredible hour – and then we heard the siren. Was it possible that it was illegal to be on the roof of the junior high school? Surely not, but we dropped to our knees and huddled together closely, holding hands with all our might. I noticed at that time that Lizzie's arm was still bleeding.

"Oh, Lizzie," I said, "I am so sorry you got hurt."

"Never mind," she replied, "but I'm scared. I hope that we aren't arrested." We heard a squawk, and then a voice from a megaphone called out loudly.

"We know you are on the roof. Come down now!" Our life was over. We just knew it. But, being the good little Christian girls that we were, we held our hands in the air and gave ourselves up. The policemen actually helped us climb down from the roof, but then they gave us a severe lecture that went on forever. I wasn't sure about Lizzie but, by the end, I was very close to throwing up. When they finally let us go, they warned us that if we were ever caught breaking the law again, we would be in big trouble.

Lizzie and I ran as fast as we could to our homes. I extracted one more promise from Lizzie that she wouldn't tell her mother how she'd gotten cut, and then we separated – each of us desperately hoping that the police hadn't ratted us out to our parents. Luck was with us. No one at home seemed to be aware of any wrongdoings committed by the girls who had guiltily slipped back into their houses. It seemed that we were going to be okay. The consequences of our sins did not appear until a day later...

It was Monday, a school day, and Lizzie was getting special help from her second grade teacher in spelling. Lizzie was favoring her right arm a bit and it hurt to hold her pencil. Her teacher told her to stretch out her arm. When she did, the teacher noticed more than a bandaged cut – she saw a dark line creeping up the vein in Lizzie's wrist.

"Lizzie," she said, "how did you get this cut?" My Lizzie, of course, would only admit to hurting herself on some metal. She never mentioned that she had an older friend who had coerced her into climbing up a rusty air conditioning unit in order to conquer the unknown wonders of the world on top of the junior high school. Lizzie's teacher quickly called the school nurse and her mom. I only learned about this much later, although I knew that something was amiss when Lizzie did not show up at the corner to wait for me after school.

Blood poisoning. I will never forget the way I felt when I was told the news by my mother.

"Lizzie was rushed to the doctor today, Bobbi," she said. "She had blood poisoning!" I immediately knew that it must have been the horrible cut on her arm that had poisoned her. Was she dying? Would I be able to tell her how sorry I was, that I loved her, and good-bye until we met again in Heaven? Finally, I understood the mumble of words that were coming out of my mother's mouth. Lizzie was okay. She was on medication, but she was home. I started to run toward the door with the question, 'Can I go and see her?' on my lips.

"Oh no you don't," my mother said. "Lizzie cannot play today. She must rest."

I was crestfallen. I was afraid to call her, knowing that her mother would answer the phone and that I, in my agony, would probably blurt out my confession in a rush of words and tears. I was certain that if I ever let anyone know I had given Lizzie blood poisoning, I would be banned from playing with her forever. And so, I suffered in silence.

☜ 2 ☞

It was 1971 and there were few distractions for kids at that time. We had a tiny little black and white TV with three fuzzy channels, two if it was windy. But most of the time, the television was off. We children were not allowed to turn it on when it was light outside.

"Go downstairs or go outside." Those were our options.

I had siblings – four of them, actually – and we knew every square foot of Richland, Washington. My sister, Angela, was a beautiful, popular fifteen-year-old. She was the only one of us kids who had brunette hair like my parents. And her eyes matched her hair. Everyone always made a fuss over how pretty Angela was, which might have made the rest of us feel jealous, but Angela was so nice, she was such a good big sister, that it was pretty much impossible not to adore her. Sometimes, when we were all stuck in the basement because it was too cold to go outside, I could convince her to play the card game, Spit, with me. She was a very good Spit player and she beat me every time, which ultimately caused me to start crying.

Angela got to the point where she would say, "I don't want to play with you because you always get mad at me and cry." I would cross my heart and hope to die.

"I won't cry this time. I promise!" And she, because she was such a love, would agree to play with me one more time. And I, because I was so competitive, would always end up crying.

Next was my brother, Graham, who was fourteen at the time. He was my idol. Graham was musical; he played the piano with such a passion that my mother knew that he was going to be the next Van Cliburn. And he could have been; only he was also a singer, and an actor, and an athlete, and the president of his class. I remember, as we got older, girls would come up and surround my mother after one or another of Graham's performances.

"Please, make Graham marry me, Mrs. Johnson," one girl would beg, while the others giggled. "We love him!" My mother would smile and bask in the reflection of her son's glory. I would usually be standing near my mother, with a proud smile on my face. For as long as I could remember, I had been known as Graham's little sister. But that never bothered me one bit.

It was common back then for all the neighborhood kids to get together in the evening to play baseball in our back yard. Graham was older than most of us, so he usually wouldn't join us, but when he did, it made the game so much more fun. I always wanted to impress him, to hit a home run so that he would notice me and maybe tell me that I was good. One time, I got up to bat, my dad was pitching, Graham was catching, and I hit the ball so hard that it went over our chain link fence. I was elated and my feet barely touched the ground as I rounded the bases. As I was heading for home, I turned to see where the ball was and somehow got off course. The next thing I remember was hitting the steel pole of the carport with my head. I fell down as if dead, so quickly had I been running. Even through my pain, I looked around for my big brother.

"Was I safe? Did I touch home plate?" That was really all that mattered to me.

"Yes, Bobbi," Graham assured me quickly. "You touched home before I caught the ball. Way to go!" I just closed my eyes and smiled. All was well. Graham had witnessed my home run.

My sister, Adele, was next in line. She was twelve. Adele had flaming red hair, or at least that's how I heard most adults describe it. Her hair was stick straight and it was so long that she could sit on it, which I thought was the coolest thing ever. As far as I was concerned, she and I were the same person. I mean, we didn't look alike; I had ash brown curly hair that seemed to stop growing once it reached my shoulders, but we felt the same way about everything, pretty much. We loved to play dolls together, and always had. No one played dolls as well as we did. Sometimes, we would let our friends bring their Barbies over and join us in our basement. But, in spite of the fact that our friends had way better Barbie stuff (Adele and I had always dreamed about getting a Barbie fold-out house for Christmas – the one with the built in closets, where you could hang up little Barbie dresses on little Barbie hangers), we always agreed, once our friends left, that they just didn't know how to play dolls as well as we did.

Adele and I were outside girls as well. Whether it was baseball in our back yard, or any organized game on the playing field during recess, we were both good athletes and we played to win. At school, boys always picked us first to be on their teams, and we rarely let them down. The thing that I loved most about Adele was that, even though she had her own friends, she was always happy to let Lizzie and me join her. She never seemed to get annoyed with us, that is, until the day that she got her period. After she crossed that milestone, Adele suddenly began to realize how interesting Angela was. I fell off her radar screen and there was no amount of 'Let's play Barbies' that could draw her back. She wanted to learn the art of being feminine from our older sister, and I lost my Adele.

I could not have been less interested in being feminine. As a matter of fact, even the word feminine made me blush. A few years earlier, I had been in the ladies' room with my sisters and my mother. I was standing in the midst of a number of women who were waiting to use the facilities. I walked around the room and stopped in front of a rectangular box hanging on the wall. It had a pretty flower painted on it. I looked up and read the elegant cursive writing.

"Oh," I said out loud, "they are selling feminine napkins in this bathroom." To my surprise, every last lady in the room burst out laughing. I didn't know why the fact that lacy handkerchiefs being available for purchase in a bathroom was so funny, but I knew well enough that I had made a complete fool of myself. I was too embarrassed even to have my mother explain it to me in the quiet of our own car.

"Never mind," I said, shaking my head vigorously. "I don't want to know." And so, when Adele joined the ranks of the feminine, I let her go. I loved to play. I was all about playing, and so I gave her up without much of a fight. No hard feelings.

I was the fourth child. Although I was two years younger than Adele, I was almost as tall as she was, something that I hated about myself. I always looked around at the short girls in my classroom and thought that they were so much cuter. And even though I was the same age as the other girls in my class, I felt like I was much older. The things that my classmates talked about seemed to be, I don't know, silly to me. I would never have let these girls know what I was secretly thinking, but I was just not like them. The only positive thing about being different, about being so tall, was that I was also athletic, which made me popular with the boys.

After me came Scottie, my baby brother. Scottie loved Lizzie almost as much as I did because he knew that – when Lizzie wasn't around – I would be looking to play with him every waking moment. Scottie and Lizzie were the same age, and I always felt that they were destined to get married, and then Lizzie and I would be sisters. When Scottie was little, he was docile, and I loved that. He would let me play make believe with him; he was Ken to my Barbie, so long as I didn't tell anyone (and why would I – and risk losing Ken?). He climbed trees with me and we played with his STP racers, and we rode all over the countryside on our Honda 50's. He was a perfect playmate until about the age of seven – and then it dawned on him just how much power he had over me.

Lizzie was known to go on long vacations over the summer, and that left me with Scottie. It became a game for him to act uninterested in the plans that I made for us on those glorious summer days. Lizzie and I had discovered that if you dug by the banks of the Columbia River, which was just a short bicycle ride away from our homes, you found oozy, wonderful clay. Before Lizzie's parents took her off to the coast, she and I had dug up pounds of clay and dragged it back home in buckets. We made clay pots, and clay kitties, and clay fruit. It was so exciting. We felt like we were real artists. We lined our creations up on a board in the back yard to let the sun bake them. Once they were ready, we planned to paint them, and then they would be perfect. We were going to sell them, of course. We just knew that our neighbors would love to own one of our beautiful clay objects. So, even though Lizzie had to leave, I wanted to keep making more and more art. But it was no fun digging by myself – I really wanted Scottie to take Lizzie's place. I asked him to ride with me to the river and help me dig up more clay and then help me lug it back home.

"Scottie," I explained, "not only will it be fun, but we'll make lots of money." I knew that if there was something in it for him, he would be more likely to say yes. But Scottie said no. He said that he thought our clay figures were stupid and that no one would ever in a million years buy them. Well, that was Scottie. I always had to make allowances for him. He wasn't the creative genius that both Lizzie and I were, so I decided to change my approach. Instead of emphasizing the money that we could make, I told him all about how much fun it was going to be at the river. I told him that everybody was hanging out at the river that summer. I told him that we could wear our swimming suits so it wouldn't be like we were there just to work. We would dig a little, and gather our buckets of clay, and then we would swim a little with our friends.

"Come on, you know that sounds like fun," I said, trying not to sound desperate. "How about it?"

"No," Scottie said. "I'm not interested in playing in the mud with you." Oh, he made me so mad! To make matters worse, in that very same mud where we would have been digging, they later discovered the ancient remains of what they called Richland Man. If only Scottie had helped me that summer, maybe we would have found those bones. We would have been famous. But it was 'no' and 'nope' and 'don't wanna'. I was so furious – I could feel the blood rush to my cheeks.

"What else do you have to do?" I asked him sternly. But he just ignored me. What I didn't realize was that the more upset I got, the more entertaining I was to my brother. This went on for years, simply years. It was so irritating.

All of us kids knew that we were not allowed to hate; we were certainly not allowed to say the words 'I hate you'. In fact, there was a verse that my mother quoted to us all the time that said if you don't love your brother, how can you say you love God? It was clear to me that if I allowed myself to feel hatred toward my brother, then I *would* go to Hell. And so, when Scottie refused to play with me, I got as close to him as I could and I said in my harshest whisper, "I love you in Jesus, Scottie, but I hate your guts!" I was pretty sure that God would give me that one. But Scottie just laughed, which drove me to the brink of insanity.

Year later, when Scottie and I were in college, he finally admitted to me that it had been his favorite thing as a kid to yank my chain. I can remember very clearly looking at my eighteen-year-old brother.

"For real?" I said incredulously, "You knew what you were doing to me? You knew how mad you were making me?" He just laughed, but this time it didn't anger me.

"Yeah, it was so funny. Your face would get beet red." Thankfully, by that time in my life I had adopted a more Lizzie-like approach to dealing with my frustrations, so, where I would have wanted to kill him just a few years earlier, on that day I just laughed.

"I knew it," I said to him. "I knew you were doing it on purpose!" And then, just because I could (after all, Mom wasn't anywhere near us) I punched his arm as hard as I could, but he just laughed.

3

When I was ten, my father received a scholarship to attend the University of Washington in Seattle. He and my mother had married five days after they graduated from high school and, consequently, my father had just started his second year of college before the babies started coming. The two years of school were enough to get him an associate's degree, which made him eligible for work out at the plant. Now, all these years later, he was given the opportunity to earn his engineering degree. And so, the seven of us packed our bags and moved to Seattle.

This was a very traumatic move for me, because it meant I had to leave my very best friend in the whole wide world. How could I live without my Lizzie? It also happened that at the same time I reached another milestone. I 'blossomed into a young woman', as the fourth grade pamphlet read – I had begun to menstruate. Okay, I couldn't even say the word because it creeped me out so much. The day it started, I was so mortified that I told no one. I was so afraid that my mom would be mad that I'd ruined my underwear. I was so shocked and angry that my body had betrayed me and turned me into a woman without my permission. And I was so completely embarrassed at the prospect of anyone else finding out, especially Lizzie (who was so young and so innocent), that I went into the bathroom by myself, found a sponge under the sink, and wrapped toilet paper around and around and around it. After few hours, however, I realized that my solution wasn't going to work. I ran into the bathroom, burst into tears, and called out to my mom for help. She thought that I had thrown up. I wished it was just that; how I longed for the simplicity of a childhood illness! She wanted me to let her into the bathroom, but I couldn't, I simply couldn't. It became obvious that I was beginning to annoy my mother, so I very quickly confessed that I had become a woman, and that I didn't know what to do about it. To my astonishment, and to my extreme embarrassment, she let out a sigh and started to laugh. She left me for a few moments, and then she came back and insisted that I let her in the bathroom. What could I do? I knew better than to say no to my mother at that point. She came in with a box of feminine napkins – the dreaded feminine napkins – and so began my life as a woman.

There I was in a new town with an entirely new body. I had always been tall for my age, but now I was developing so quickly,

I barely recognized myself. I refused to discuss these changes with the female members of my family. I felt sure that they found my physical changes amusing; that they were talking about me behind my back. It wasn't that the girls in my family were mean-spirited, they were just so very blasé and open about topics that I found to be so deeply personal. I tried very hard not to make eye contact with them. My mom would not allow me to wear a bra yet – I was too young. So I took to wearing loose shirts and slouching a little bit; hoping to disguise my 'mountains', as my little brother called them.

Scottie had become a very important part of my life once we moved to Seattle. For one thing, he and I shared a bedroom. We slept on bunk beds; I got the top bunk, of course, and he was below me. Our bedroom was also my father's office. It was a long and narrow room in which our bed was pushed up against one wall and our dad's desk was pushed up against the other wall. He had to shuffle and squeeze in order to get into his chair. Every night, he would study into the wee hours of the morning while Scottie and I snuggled into our many blankets, trying to keep warm. We always felt safe and secure in our beds, with the green glow of Daddy's desk lamp acting as a night light.

We lived in a rented house within the Seattle city limits. There was actually a sign that said 'Seattle City Limits' on our very own street. Somehow that made me feel very, I don't know, sophisticated or something. Considering Richland had a population of about twenty-five thousand people at the time, Seattle, with over half a million people, was a very big city indeed.

Our house was old, but it was big and sprawling and architecturally very interesting. It had a large stone fireplace that seemed to grow out of the floor. The room that Scottie and I shared was on the other side of the fireplace. It was quite obviously an add-on, because the back of the fireplace protruded into it. I loved having those large stones as a wall in our room. As Scottie and I fell asleep each night, I would talk about how cool it would be if we could burrow through those large boulders and get into the big part of the house. There would be a secret passageway that no one but he and I would know about. We would press a button and the back of the fireplace would open up, and there it would be, our very own private entrance into the house. There was always a tunnel and it was always exciting – like something out of a *Hardy Boys* book – filled with mystery and intrigue.

By the age of nine, I had already decided that I was going to be a sleuth when I grew up. I would be like Joe Hardy, not Nancy Drew. Nancy Drew was such a girl. No, I was going to be Joe Hardy, fearless, brave, and most of all, impetuous. I had read every *Hardy Boys* book that had ever been written, some of them more than once. The *Hardy Boys* were terribly exciting. They allowed me to travel to New York, to Brazil, and to Peru. Every book started by describing the principal characters. Frank, the oldest, dark-haired brother, was practical, reliable, someone to depend upon. Joe, on the other hand, was full of life. He loved adventure. He was impetuous. Every *Hardy Boys* book described Joe as being impetuous. I loved that word. I wanted to be that word – impetuous.

Joe was a Hardy, so he was reputable. He was a good boy, a boy of great character, but he had urges that drove him to do things that maybe Frank just wouldn't have done; but, in the end, the mysteries wouldn't have been solved without Joe's passion. Frank always acknowledged that it was Joe's instincts that inevitably led them to find the culprit. I'm not sure that Scottie ever actually felt the great, stirring passion in his heart that I was left feeling in mine after finishing each and every one of those exhilarating books, but he read them anyway, and we had that in common.

Poor Scottie, he was sweet enough to listen to me while I talked on and on about how amazing it would be if we had a secret tunnel, or maybe even a spiral staircase that led to – who knows what – maybe an attic full of old treasures?

I guess that I was a bit of a dreamer. There is no doubt that I was an optimist. I believed that if a person was selfless; if she was full of dreams that only God could place in her heart and soul – she would be able to accomplish great things – things that would prevail beyond her own lifetime. As it turns out, during the years that I spent in Seattle, my faith would be shaken to the core. I had grown up believing that right would always win out; that purity, wholesomeness, and unconditional love would always bring safety and happiness to one's life. Circumstances would soon force me to face the fact that evil existed, even in my perfect world.

It went against every nice, happily-ever-after story that I had ever read. It went against every wonderful show that ended with a kiss that I had ever seen. I had been taught that if I didn't look for trouble, then I would be able to avoid it. I discovered that no one was exempt from the darkness that existed on this earth. It crept into even the lightest, most unlikely places in the world. I found that out one day when I wasn't looking.

4

My first encounter with the ugly side of life came when I was asked to babysit the little boy across the street. His name was Nicky, and he was a cute little kid. So what if I was only ten; I was very mature for my age. Plus, I could easily see my mom from Nicky's back yard. Usually, she was standing at our kitchen counter, baking cookies. If anything went wrong, all I had to do was cry out for help; she would be able to hear me through our kitchen window.

The first time that I babysat, Nicky and I played in his yard for a little while, and then he wanted a snack. I took him inside to make him a peanut butter and jelly sandwich, only to discover that there was no peanut butter.

"My mom keeps the peanut butter downstairs," Nicky told me. So I went down into the basement in search of the pantry. It was a dark, dank basement, as basements in Seattle tended to be, and the only light that I could see was a bulb hanging from the center of the room with a string on it. I quickly pulled the string and then was able to see a row of shelves that had cans and jars of food lined up on them. I ran my eyes over every shelf, but I did not see any peanut butter, so I carefully felt my way down a dark hallway to see if there were more shelves somewhere else. I felt something rub across my face which made me scream, and then I realized that it was just another string to a light. I pulled it, and when the light was on, I saw that I was at the other end of the basement in a little hall. There were more shelves on the back wall; most were filled with jars of canned fruit, but there was a big can on the top shelf that looked like it could have been peanut butter. I had to step on a lower shelf in order to reach the can, and when I did the entire wall moved in like it was a door.

That was cool. I couldn't help but wonder what was behind the moving shelves; it looked like it might lead into a closet, but maybe it was a secret passageway. Maybe the passageway went under the street and connected to my house! I was excited as I pushed the heavy door in – there was a glow coming from behind it. I stopped pushing and made my way around the shelves. When I peeked in I saw that it was a room, not a passageway, and I was kind of disappointed. But still, it was a *secret* room, something I had only read about in books. I simply had to explore it. I glanced over my shoulder to see if Nicky had followed me. I didn't want him to tell his parents that I was snooping around their house. He wasn't there, so I pushed my way farther into the room. As my eyes adjusted to the dark, I looked around. What I saw made me gasp and I quickly slammed my eyes shut. I backed my way out of the room and once I was on the other side, I pulled on the shelf-door with all my might. It clicked shut. I tried to push it open again, but it wouldn't budge. Apparently, it had locked when I pulled it shut. I quickly reached and pulled the light off and ran back into the main room. What I had seen hanging on every wall in that dark little room were dozens of pictures of naked ladies. I was so shaken up that I couldn't remember why I had gone downstairs in the first place. When I emerged at the top of the stairs, Nicky asked me where the peanut butter was.

"We're going to have crackers and cheese instead," I said. I wondered if Nicky even knew about his father's disgusting secret. I never mentioned it to him. In fact, there were very few people who I talked to about that room, until… but I will get to that later.

I didn't like to think about nasty stuff and I was good at tuning it out and closing my eyes to it. So that's what I did – if I didn't think about it, it wasn't there. What was difficult for me was that Nicky and his parents thought that I was the best babysitter ever, so I had to go over to the Anderson's house all the time, but I never looked directly at Mr. Anderson again. In spite of how hard I tried not to think about it, his secret had opened up some scary place in my soul. It frightened me, especially because I couldn't talk about it with anyone. I began to develop other fears too. I hated to be outside at night. If I was coming home from a friend's by myself after dark, I would jump behind a tree when a car came, and wait until the headlights faded away. Then, I'd make a dash for home, fleeing – I don't know what exactly.

Of course, this was the height of the hippy era, and there were some pretty odd-looking people roaming around Seattle – people we would never have seen in Richland at that time. I would overhear my dad telling my mom about some of his classmates and how they were always talking about marijuana, LSD, and rock-and-roll music. Before we moved to Seattle, a really good local electric guitarist had just died a young death. He was drunk or high one night and they said he drowned in his own vomit. Sad and gross, I thought. It seemed strange to me, because I had never even heard of Jimi Hendrix until after his death, then everybody was talking about him. People said it was tragic because he could have been really great, but in a few years he would probably be forgotten.

My father was a full-time student at the University of Washington. That was his job during those years that we lived in Seattle. I thought that it was pretty cool that he was getting paid to go to school, and I wished that somebody would pay me to go to school. One day he took all of us to an open house of sorts on the campus at the university. There we all were, ranging in age from eight to sixteen. We went to my father's English class and the professor turned off all the lights to show us a short, creative film that he had produced. The music came on; I will never forget it:

Here comes the sun... Here comes the sun and I say,

It's all right, to do oo oo, do oo oo, do oo oo, do do do do

On the screen was a beautiful sunrise, reflecting off of the ocean. We all settled in to enjoy the short film, and then, right in the middle of the glorious sunrise appeared a wet, curvaceous blonde who was totally naked. She was spread out on a blanket on the beach, apparently enjoying the sun on her body. I didn't see anything else because I, of course, instantly shut my eyes – icky feelings spreading all over my body. My dad immediately jumped out of his seat.

"Children, let's go!" he ordered, and all five Johnson children scrambled to follow him out of the room. A long-haired student wearing a leather headband looked at my dad and shook his head.

"What's the matter, Man?" he said. "It's a beautiful thing." But Dad ignored him and focused on getting us out. We never talked about it. My poor father, I'm sure that he felt like he had defiled his precious children. I'm not sure what effect that experience had on my siblings, but I did, in fact, feel dirty or guilty or some other bad feeling that I couldn't quite put my finger on.

There were other reasons to be afraid as well. I always took a shortcut home from my elementary school through the woods. Sometimes Scottie walked with me, but sometimes he ran away from me, just to make me mad. It was one of those days, when Scottie was far ahead of me, that I heard him yell.

"Bobbi," he cried, "over here." I ran up to where he was standing and looked to see what he'd found. There, next to what looked like a campfire site, were a pair of panties and a bra.

"Scottie!" I said, and I grabbed him and tried to clamp my hand over his eyes. "Don't look at that." He tried to pull away from me, but I was bigger than he was, and I forced him to run all the way home with me. Later that night, Scottie, from his bottom bunk, wasn't his usual silent self.

"Do you think they burned her body at the campsite?" he whispered. "I wonder why we didn't hear about this on the news?" I had been thinking the same thing: her bra and panties were there; what had happened to the girl? Something awful – I was sure. After that experience, Scottie and I discovered other articles of clothing left in random places all over the same area. We came to those woods almost every day after school because that's where the best trails for riding mini bikes were.

We never told our parents about the underwear and other clothes that we found there, but one day – and I wasn't sure what caused them to do this – they told us that we were not allowed to take the shortcut through the woods anymore. Neither Scottie nor I put up much of a protest, even though it meant that it would take us ten minutes longer to get home every day, and we would also be losing our favorite mini bike trails. These things didn't matter because the truth was, we were getting scared of those woods.

Thankfully, not everything in Seattle was scary and bad. We had been living there for over a year, and during that year, I had finally met a boy who was taller than I was, Jimmy Gilbert. We were in the fourth grade so we still had recess at school. Jimmy was a real jock and he was always chosen to be one of the captains of whatever sport we were playing during our time outside: kickball, baseball, or dodge ball. The captains would, of course, pick the athletic guys first, but once the wimpy boys and the girls were all that were left, Jimmy would always pick me. That made me feel so special. Jimmy was taller than I was and he was cute and, at that time in my life, that's all it took. I was in love. He had blonde, curly hair and green eyes. Every time I saw him, I wanted to sigh. But I didn't, of course. For Christmas that year, Miss Nelson had us put our names in a hat to pick out our Secret Santas. I have no recollection of who I picked, but as it turned out, Jimmy got my name. It couldn't have been an accident because I had been secretly praying that God would make Jimmy notice me, you know, as a girl – not just a teammate. I will never forget what he gave me; it was a gigantic, three-inch thick candy cane.

I loved that candy cane. I wouldn't open it – I never did – even after the plastic wrapping yellowed and cracked apart. His sweet offering secured my heart. I planned to save it forever. After receiving his gift, I wanted to show Jimmy how I felt about him, but I didn't have an inkling as to how to do it. It wasn't until spring that I came up with an idea that, to me, seemed very romantic. I decided that I would gather wild daisies and tie them together with a string and leave them on his front porch.

And so I did. I picked the biggest bunch of daisies that I could hold, and took them home to find a string. The problem was that daisies really didn't smell very good. I couldn't give Jimmy a bouquet of flowers that stunk! Fortunately, everyone was occupied, so I was able to sneak into Angela's room. She had a bottle of perfume with a soft, fuzzy, leopard skin top. I loved that bottle of perfume. I would always pet the fuzzy cap whenever I went in to her room. Angela and Adele were in the living room, singing *Daydream Believer* at the top of their lungs, so I knew that I was safe. I quickly grabbed the perfume and ran out of the house with it. I unscrewed the top of the bottle and liberally sprinkled Oil of Musk all over my daisies. I then tied the daises together in a bundle, and headed over to Jimmy's house.

I had to ride my bike because it would have taken me too long to walk, but, luckily, I had a basket on my bike, so I put my bouquet of daisies into the basket, and sailed off. I was so happy. It was a beautiful spring day and I was in love. I rode with no hands, and even closed my eyes. Life could not have been better. Once I got close to Jimmy's house, I hid my bike down the road, grabbed my daisies, and ran from tree to tree until I was in his front yard. I slipped up onto his porch, placed the daisies on his front mat, and rang the doorbell. Then I ran like the wind.

I got to my bicycle without looking back and rode with all of my might back to my home. Once home, I climbed my favorite tree. The tree was actually a landmark in our area. It was enormous – the perfect climbing tree with low, fat limbs and a smooth bark that felt good to lay your face against. The five of us thought it was a perfect place to build a tree house in, and so we did, nailing scrap pieces of wood into the smooth bark with complete abandon. Our landlords saw what we had done to their tree one day, and I remember them yelling at my parents! Oops –

we didn't know how valuable the tree was. But the damage was already done, so they didn't make us take our fort down. The other kids eventually grew tired of the tree house, but not me. I would have slept in it if my parents had let me. So, that's where I was when I heard my sister Angela call my name.

"Bobbi," she said, "were you playing with my perfume?" Yikes. I had forgotten to put the leopard bottle back on my sister's dresser. How could I have been so stupid?

"What?" I said, desperately trying to think of a reason that I would have brought her bottle of perfume outside.

"Bobbi, I know what you did," she said. What did she mean, she knew what I did? I lay in my tree house hoping against hope that Angela would just go away. "Jimmy's mother just called." Noooooo, this could not be happening. How could Jimmy's mother have known that it was me who left the daisies on the front mat?

"I don't know what you are talking about, Angela," I said breathlessly.

"It's okay, Bobbi. She's not mad, and I'm not mad that you used my perfume." Oh, how I wanted to die. Nice as it was that Angela was being so sweet to me, I would have rather walked through flames than to have to go through the humiliation of being caught in the act of playing out one of my romantic dreams. "She thinks it was kind of cute," Angela continued. "I do too, Bobbi – I didn't even think you knew that boys existed."

By that time I was crying. I pulled my shirt up to my face to muffle my tears, but I was simply beside myself with embarrassment. Angela must have heard my sobs because she climbed up into the tree house to be with me. To this day, I feel badly about the way I treated Angela that afternoon. She was being so kind, when she could have been terribly, terribly angry at me for taking her personal belongings. But she crawled up next to me and said, "Don't be embarrassed, Bobbi. I think it's adorable that you have a crush on a boy."

"I do not have a crush on a boy!" I said in my meanest voice. "I don't know what you are talking about. Just leave me alone!" And after a minute, she did. She climbed back down out of the tree, and we never talked about that incident again. Stupid, stupid little girl I was...

Between Jimmy's home and mine was an old abandoned house that was a favorite place for Scottie and me to explore. It was kind of scary, which was part of the fun. There were broken steps out front, and actual holes in the wooden floors inside. We would pretend that we were on a case, looking for the stolen gold that the bad guys had stashed in the house until it was safe for them to come back for it. They had been caught and put in prison, but one of them left a note pointing to that very house as the place of concealment. We found the note and were moments away from discovering the gold. We tippy-toed like Indians as we went from one room to the next, just in case one of the thugs had escaped and returned for his loot. We loved this game and looked forward to it every Saturday.

It was one of those Saturdays, and Scottie and I had just finished our chores – or, I should say, I had finished my chores. Scottie, after all, was the baby in the family, and he was a boy. What could he be expected to do around the house for my mom? But I had folded the clothes and put them away, and dusted and vacuumed the living room, so I was free, completely free, and it was only eleven o'clock in the morning. We were excited to head over to the Haunted Mansion, as we liked to call it, for another afternoon of adventure. As we got close to it, we heard noises coming from inside.

"Shhh – Scottie, come over here," I said, and I quickly pulled him behind an overgrown shrub. We were very still as we listened for what seemed like hours, trying to figure out who was in our house. From the sound of it, there was a group of people inside. And, after a while, we detected a funny smell wafting out of the front door; kind of a sweet, smoky smell, but it wasn't cigarettes. The longer we stayed, the louder they got. Apparently, something was very funny, because they were all laughing hysterically. And then we heard a shriek, and a girl came bounding out of the house.

Scottie and I bunched ourselves into little balls so as not to be detected, and soon four more people came tumbling out of the house.

"Ewwww!" one of the girls screamed, "was that a rat or a mouse?"

"I think it was a rat, Man. Did you see that thing? Can you say huge?" It was a group of teenage hippies; they were laughing and falling all over themselves.

"Come on," one of them said, "let's go to the cave."

Scottie and I looked at each other excitedly. A cave? Right in the middle of the city? Without saying a word to each other, we began to follow the hippies from a distance as they laughed and staggered and zigzagged through the woods. Right before they got to our back yard, they turned into the overgrown brush to the right of our property. Scottie and I had never gone in there because it was just a bunch of weeds and pine trees, but the teenagers seemed to be very familiar with those woods. We stayed way back so that they wouldn't discover us, and after a while we couldn't hear them anymore.

"Where do you think they went?" I asked Scottie. He just shrugged and started to make his way into the woods. "Be careful, Scottie," I said. But I was right behind him. We had only gone about twenty feet when we came upon a hole in the earth. We looked at each other in amazement. Talk about an adventure. We knew better than to go into the hole while the teenagers were in there, so we sneaked back out of the woods and stealthily made our way back home and climbed into our tree house.

"It really is a cave!" I said. "Can you believe it? We have to go back there and explore!" Our lives had never seemed more exciting than on that Saturday afternoon. We waited and waited until we were sure that the hippies had left, and then we headed back. I'm not sure about Scottie, but I was so scared, I was afraid I was going to wet my pants.

We made our way to the hole in the ground and listened long and hard. When we were absolutely sure that there was nobody inside, we dropped to our knees and crawled into the cave. It turned out to be a long tunnel, and there were candles that were still lit as we got deeper and deeper into the earth. We finally got to the end, where it opened up; it was probably ten feet by ten feet. It had a bunch of candles that were burning, and there were pillows and blankets and burned-out sticks of incense scattered all around. In the middle of the cave we saw a Zippo lighter and a couple of funny looking pipes lying in a pile of ashes.

Scottie and I looked at each other, and we both saw fear upon the other's face – drugs! I think it occurred to both of us at the same time that the hippies would probably be coming back soon, so we started to scramble out of there like our lives depended on it. Thankfully, we ran into no one, and once we got to the end of the tunnel, we made a beeline for home. We never returned to that site of adventure again because we knew that if we had been caught by the teenagers, we probably wouldn't have ever seen the light of day again.

Later that year, someone bought that plot of land and began to clear the trees. Once they had cut them all down, they brought a big earthmover to dig out the roots, and as the machine moved over where the cave was, the earth gave way under the weight of it. The driver was fine, but the earthmover was stuck in a cock-eyed position for an entire day while construction men tried to figure a way to pull it out.

Scottie and I finally felt like it was safe to tell about our discovery earlier in the year. Our big brother and sisters thought that we were very cool to have discovered an actual cave near our own back yard.

"And it was a cave that was used for nefarious reasons, even," Graham remarked.

Scottie and I looked at each other. He shrugged and I shrugged back. We had no idea what *nefarious* meant, but we both looked at Graham with big smiles on our faces and nodded our heads in agreement.

6

I spoke of my fears before, because fear, for me, was a new thing. I had always prided myself on not being afraid or, at least, on being very good at disguising my fear. But something about the big city of Seattle, the sudden changes that I was forced to go through physically, and the creepy discoveries that I was making about people who lived very, very near what I considered to be 'safe' – like in the game *tag:* 'This is safe! You can't get me here, I'm on safe!' – combined to make me aware of a very unsettled feeling in the pit of my stomach.

Lucky for me, I received the news that Lizzie was going to be allowed to spend the entire month of June and some of July with me in Seattle! In exactly twenty-six days, Lizzie would be arriving on my doorstep – I could hardly contain myself. I noticed that my mother was requiring that I spend a lot of time out-of-doors. Possibly it was because I had gotten into the habit of asking the same question eight and nine times a day.

"Lizzie's mom said she could come, right? She's really going to spend most of the summer with us, right?"

I had developed insomnia that spring. I simply could not fall asleep. The harder I tried, the wider-eyed I'd become. At first, my mother let me sleep with her and Daddy. I loved that. They had a great big bed, and it was so warm – much warmer than my top bunk. But, as much as I loved being in between my mom and dad, I still could not fall asleep, and I tossed and turned, pulling the covers here and there. Finally, my parents decided that the arrangement was not working. My mother moved me to the couch. She told me it was in my best interest. In order to help me fall asleep, she tied a string to the chain on the light. The string reached all the way to the couch, so I didn't even have to get out of bed to turn it off. When I felt like my eyes were just about to close, I would pull the string. My insomnia was so bad that my mother did not even tell me that I had to shut off the light at a certain time.

"Read," she instructed, "for as long as you want..." She really must have been desperate, because my mother was a get-with-the-program kind of woman. She did not readily make allowances for our petty needs. But my sleeping problem was an issue that was taking a toll on the entire family, and she wanted to fix me as quickly as possible. The couch was my bed for three months, and when my mom asked me how it was going, I told her 'fine' because I didn't want her to get mad at me. But one night, she came out of her room and caught me reading at two o'clock in the morning. The next thing I knew, she had put me in Adele's room.

Adele wanted to be a doctor from the time that she could walk, and she was very good at healing people. I don't know what my mother said to Adele about me, but Adele took it upon herself to make the boogeyman in my life go away. She rubbed my back and told me stories and chanted little hypnotic songs until I eventually gave up the ghost, but the minute she stopped her incantations, my eyes snapped back open. I was miserable, and I knew that I was making everyone else in the family miserable too. The thing that made my problem almost unbearable was the fact that everyone in the family knew that I had a problem. I was such a deeply private person, but my inability to fall asleep was making me so anxious that I simply could not hide my fears. We never spoke about my problem out loud, but I was aware that everybody knew.

Finally, after sleeping in my parents' bed and sleeping on the couch hadn't worked, and Adele hadn't been able to cure me, my mother, in desperation, took me to a doctor. We didn't have the money to go to a doctor, but she was determined to get to the bottom of my insomnia. Mother liked everything in her family to be ship-shape, and my lack of sleep was rocking the boat. It was time to take me to a professional.

In the meantime, I was truly in a state of self-loathing. What in the world was wrong with me? I just wanted it to be all over soon. I hated being a nuisance. The doctor came in and did a thorough exam, and his prognosis would forever resonate in my memory. I was sitting on the examination table, wearing a thin paper shirt that opened in the front, listening to the doctor talk to my mother. I held my arms clutched around my chest, and I was swinging my crossed legs back and forth to the beat of a song I had just learned on the piano. The doctor looked at me, shook his head, and made a little 'tsk-tsk' noise with his tongue.

"This is a very nervous child," he said to my mother. "I really don't know what to say." And with that, he turned and left the room. My mother was so angry. She muttered to herself in the car all the way back home.

"I paid fifteen dollars to be told that my daughter is nervous? Well, thank you very much – I had already picked up on that!"

Thank goodness, a few days later, Lizzie came, and the very first night she was there, I fell asleep the minute my head hit the pillow. I was a very happy little girl again.

7

It was the summer of 1972, and life could not have been better. Lizzie was with me and we had a whole big world just waiting to be explored. I had determined in my heart to make the most of our seven weeks together.

My whole family had gone together to the Sea-Tac airport to pick her up. We arrived at the airport early to be sure that we were there when Lizzie got off the plane, so we had about an hour to kill, and my parents let Scottie and me go explore the airport for a while.

"Just stay together," my mom called out as we scampered away. Scottie and I were excited. There were escalators to ride on, something that we did not have in Richland, and so we ran over to them and took them up and then took them down. We really wanted to try running up and then back down the up escalator, but there were too many people in our way. I had gotten ahead of Scottie by slipping past a mother who was trying to convince her child to step on to the moving stairs. Poor Scottie was stuck behind them. Once I got to the top, I decided to wait until he caught up with me. I was wearing a new striped tank top that my mom had just bought for me on sale at the Sears on Aurora Avenue and a pair of cute shorts that I borrowed from Adele. I turned around to look out the window at the huge planes and, as I was turning back to see where Scottie was, a man was standing in my way. He was very close to me, so close that I could see the weave in his navy blue sweater vest. I tried to get around him but he stepped to the side. At first I was embarrassed, like it was my fault that I was in his way, but as I attempted to step around him, he reached up and grabbed my breast and squeezed it. He then pushed me out of his way and hurried on. I just stood there. I couldn't think, I couldn't move. I put my arms across my chest and I was hugging myself when Scottie came running up to me.

"What's the matter?" he asked me. I didn't say anything. "Bobbi, what's wrong with you?" Scottie tugged at my arm.

Why had I worn a tank top? What had I been thinking? I just wanted to get Lizzie and go home. I watched as Scottie started going back down the other escalator.

"Come on," he said, shaking his head. "We don't have all day." Suddenly, I realized that under no circumstances was I going to let Scottie or anyone else in the world find out about what had just happened to me. I rubbed my burning eyes and I ran after him. We only had a few minutes before we had to go back to the terminal where my family was sitting, waiting for Lizzie.

By the time we got back there, I had pulled myself together and no one, not even Scottie, could tell that anything was wrong. Then I saw Lizzie, and instantly I was a little girl again. I was so excited that I hugged her and I hugged her and I didn't want to let her go. We went to get her luggage and I never once dropped her hand.

Now that Lizzie was here, everything was going to be just the way it had always been. Everything would be perfect. I was determined to show Lizzie all of the things in Seattle that I thought that she would love to see. I wanted to make her comfortable in this new world that had become mine. But, my dad said that we should get Lizzie home and get a good meal into her. "Traveling is hard on a body," he declared.

I told Lizzie all about Highland Terrace Elementary, and how I could see the snowy peak of Mt. Rainier from my classroom window. I also told her all about our house, and the Haunted Mansion, and about the great mini bike trails throughout Seattle. I told her about everything that I found to be interesting and happy. Lizzie, ever true to her sweet, easy-going self, was totally interested and completely excited to hear all that I had to say. And she wanted to see whatever it was that I wanted to show her.

The first thing we did after we ate was to get our Honda 50's out of the garage. "Lizzie," I said, "if you thought the trails that we rode on in Richland were fun, then you will die over the trails that Scottie and I have found here." Lizzie's eyes were wide with excitement, which was all I needed.

"Let's go!" she cried. And so Lizzie and I took off on our little mini bikes. We went all over our yard, and up and down our street, and then, for some reason, I took Lizzie to the area of town where Scottie and I had been forbidden to go: the woods where we had found all the clothing. Before Lizzie had arrived, I would have been afraid to have gone back into those woods where we had seen the abandoned clothing, but now everything seemed safe again. Nothing seemed scary, so I took her to the very best trails that Scottie and I had ever discovered.

We were best friends and we were looking for an adventure. What could possibly go wrong in our lives? And so we rode on the trails in those terrifying woods. We rode until we were exhausted. The forest was truly vast. It was so much fun riding together. We pretended that we had been born a hundred years earlier and that we were riding horses over the heather-strewn landscape of England. We were the Brontë sisters, Charlotte and Emily, creating exciting and imaginary worlds. We were fearless, we were strong, we had little adult supervision, and we were having the time of our lives.

It may seem like my parents were a little reckless, giving us so much freedom, never really knowing what we were doing or where we were. But life in that day and age for us kids was pretty simple. We did our chores, practiced our instruments, and then we were told to go outside and play. We were encouraged to explore the world around us, and free to roam about all day long – so long as we weren't late for dinner.

After I showed Lizzie our trails, I showed her the Haunted Mansion, our tree fort and the other tree that was great for swinging on. I took her to Jimmy's block and pointed out his house, very carefully, lest he see us, and then I showed her my school. And at that point, I ran out of things to show her. I was a little bit worried that Lizzie might begin to feel bored and want to go home. And, there was a moment when she did, in fact, begin to show signs of being lonely for her family. But her melancholy lasted only for a few hours. Once my mother picked up on Lizzie's burgeoning homesickness, she made a phone call to her uncle who lived about a half-hour away, near the waterfront.

Uncle Roy came over that evening in his blue and white police car. Uncle Roy worked for the Seattle Police Department, the SPD. He was really nice and really handsome. I mean, he was old and everything – Lizzie said that he had just turned thirty – but he wasn't married and he loved his nieces and nephews and their friends. He took Lizzie and Scottie and me for a ride in his car, and he even played the siren and made the lights go on. Scottie and I already thought that crime-solving was the best job in the world, and now we knew firsthand that it was. It was so exciting. We were hoping that all of our friends could tell it was us in the police car. Scottie was bouncing up and down in the back seat, waving to anyone and everyone we passed. Uncle Roy finally had to tell him to settle down.

I gave my little brother a stern look and said, "Scottie!" I was so afraid that Uncle Roy would never take us for a ride again. Scottie's face kind of drooped when I yelled at him, and I felt a little bad. But Uncle Roy got all nice again, so everything was all right.

Lizzie and Scottie and I were happier than we had ever been. Uncle Roy promised to come back at least once a week to check up on us. We shouted our good-byes to him that night as he drove away, never thinking for a moment that something would happen that would require him to come back before a week's time – something that would have nothing to do with Lizzie feeling homesick. What happened four days later, on the third of June, overshadowed anyone's trivial feelings of melancholy; it was so awful, so unforeseen as to make anything that had ever happened in the past seem insignificant.

My sister Angela did not come home...

Angela. My oldest sibling, Angela, was the kind of child that any parents would be thrilled to have as their own. Angela was responsible. She was caring. She was helpful and giving and warm, and the perfect big sister. I had spent time with other families, and I'd met lots of big brothers and sisters who were really mean to us younger kids. Angela wasn't like that, not even to me, her baby sister. I knew that I probably bugged Angela, but she never let on. She was patient and kind to me – just thinking about how nice she always was gave me a big lump in my throat.

For some reason, I always acted younger than my age around Angela. I guess it was because she babied me, and I kind of liked that. With five kids, our mom didn't have time to baby anybody. Well, maybe Scottie a little bit. But when my mom was busy doing mom stuff, Angela seemed to have all the time in the world for me.

I already described our Spit matches, and I guess they really captured the relationship I had with Angela. If I had been her, I would have killed me. But not Angela; for some reason, she never seemed to tire of giving me one more chance. Most of the time, I wouldn't take advantage of her niceness. I would just walk away with my shoulders slumped, letting her beg me to play one more time and not to be sad. But sometimes, I would agree to play again, and once in a while – somehow – I would even manage to win. At those times, I would forget myself and would throw my arms around her.

"You didn't let me win, did you?"

"Of course not," she would always reply. "You just needed to get warmed up." My sister was as close to an angel as any human being has ever been. In fact, when I was little, I used to think that that was why my parents called her Angela. And so, when she did not come home that day, we were all scared out of our minds. Angela would never, ever, do something that would cause anyone to worry. She was always so aware of other people's feelings that she over-compensated when it came to letting our parents know where she was and what she was doing. So, when it got to be late on June third and Angela had not gotten home, everybody in the Johnson family took notice.

Life up until that point had felt pretty safe. My brother and Lizzie and I could freely roam all over King County without a care. But now, that same area seemed threatening and dangerous. Where was Angela? It was six-thirty and then seven and then eight and nine and ten, and still Angela had not come home. What was going on? What had gone wrong?

The first thing that happened on June third that was completely terrifying – and yet was the excitement of our community for miles around – was that the Haunted Mansion caught on fire. Lizzie and Scottie and I were over at Nicky's playing on his tire swing when we first heard the sirens. Sirens were common in Seattle; in fact, the constant sound of them in the big city was one of the first things that I noticed as being different from life in the little town of Richland. But that afternoon, as the sirens got closer and closer, and louder and louder, we stopped what we were doing, and ran to the edge of Nicky's yard. It was then that Scottie noticed the smoke.

"Whoa, I think the Haunted Mansion is on fire!" he yelled. I ran out of the gate, into the middle of the street, and then stopped, afraid to go any farther. All I could think was 'Impossible. That's our hangout – it belongs to us'. And yet, sure enough, when I finally got to the edge of our yard and looked toward the mansion, I could clearly see the smoke billowing out of the windows. By then our family had joined us outside. My father, who had just gotten home from class, began to make his way toward the burning building and we all followed him. We had not gone very far before we began to feel the heat emanating from the fire.

"That fire is not going to be stopped," my dad said. We all just stood there, along with about twenty other people, maybe more, watching the flames lick up that old, dry house. At first, the fire was only inside the house, with the flames just peeking out of the windows, but soon we could see the fire crawl out of the windows along the clapboard siding, up to the many gables of the roofline, until finally all of the shingles on the roof were alive with flames. The noise of the fire was as scary as the sight of it. It roared. I had never before considered what a fire would sound like. But now I knew. It was loud like crashing waves of the ocean, but there were also groans and creaks as the wood buckled and finally gave way with a whoosh. I could not take my eyes off of the flaming framework. It was awesome to behold and yet it was horrible at the same time, and in spite of the heat that it was giving off, I was shaking all over. The roof finally grew weak and we all watched as one gable after the other fell into the depths of the house. I couldn't look away. The fire department made a good effort, but it soon became their purpose to make sure that the fire did not spread to any of the other dwellings in the area. They sprayed down the lawns and the trees, even as they kept a steady stream of water on the old Haunted Mansion.

Eventually, my mother decided that maybe it wasn't such a good idea for us kids to be watching such devastation happen right before our eyes. She told us we had to go home. Scottie and Lizzie and I walked backwards. We felt a certain allegiance to the old place and we didn't want to let her down by leaving her. I realized as I was getting farther and farther away that my eyes were filled with tears. In fact, they were spilling down my face. I mopped them away before anyone noticed.

It was later on that same day that Angela didn't come home. She just didn't come home.

The burnt skeletal structure of our old Haunted Mansion would always remind me of the horror of that day. As it turned out, the fire department had been able to douse the fire before the entire house was completely obliterated. What was left was one standing gable, blackened and charred, but still standing.

Later, after school was back in session, I would walk past the mansion on my way to and on my way home from school every day, and I could see the scorched gable on my right in the morning and on my left in the afternoon. Day after day, I walked past the mansion, and day after day my eyes locked in on that gable. I couldn't seem to help myself. I stared at the charred remains of the mansion even though looking at it made me feel desperately sad. I kept my eyes on it until it was far enough away that I could no longer see it. I hated to see that sight every morning and every afternoon, but I could not prevent my eyes from seeking it out and staring at it.

Eventually, I took to placing my hand against the side of my face, to shield my eyes from seeing what had now become to me a sign of evil. In the morning, I would hold my right hand against my face, kind of like a horse blinder; and in the afternoon, I would place my left hand against my face. I was simply not strong enough to keep my gaze from wandering over to the blackened ruins without the help of my shielding hands.

I was never so glad as the day that the men came and completely bulldozed the mansion flat. It didn't happen until the spring of the next year, and I felt like a burden had been taken off of me. The darkness of that winter – and everything bad that had happened before that winter – was behind me, and now I could try to begin to live again.

When I thought about it, nothing really bad had ever happened to us before, outside of the fact that my grandma died when I was seven, and our dog was hit by a car right before we moved to Seattle. Those were very bad things, but we knew that old people die and that accidents happen. This bad thing – the disappearance of our beautiful, innocent Angela – seemed neither natural nor accidental.

Even so, my parents were not quick to call the police that evening because they still assumed that there was a logical explanation for Angela's absence. At first, my mom called Michelle, Angela's best friend, and Michelle said that she thought that she had seen Angela get on the bus that afternoon after cheerleading practice. Angela and four of her very best friends had made the cheerleading squad that year. They had been practicing all spring and would continue to practice all summer long so that they would be ready to cheer the boys on come fall.

After Michelle, Mom called Theresa and Phyllis and Joanne, and not one of them could think of anything that Angela said that might have indicated that she wouldn't be getting home at the regular time.

Angela worked at the Burger King down the street from us and around the corner. Mom thought that she must've gotten home from practice, changed into her uniform, and then run over to work. That's the first place that she thought to look when Angela didn't show up, so she had Graham jump on his Schwinn Sting-Ray and bike over to the Burger King to see if Angela had been asked to work late. Graham was only too happy to run over to the Burger King because he really liked a pretty blonde-haired girl named Stacey White who worked there too. When Graham finally returned home after seven, alone, my mom was furious that he hadn't let her know right away that he hadn't found Angela.

"When I saw that she wasn't there," Graham explained, "I just figured she took the shortcut home through the back yards. Sorry." My mom could never really stay mad at Graham; she was more just worried that Angela hadn't been there. She was mad at Angela. I was getting mad at Angela too. Didn't she know how anxious she was making us? And we were starved. We usually ate right around six o'clock, but our mom decided to wait for Angela to get home, and then she didn't get home and that's when all the hubbub started, so my mom never even put dinner on the table.

Mom wanted us out of the kitchen. She told us that we needed to do our homework (completely forgetting that it was summertime) and that if we didn't have any homework, then we should clean our rooms. We didn't cross my mom when she started to get into her commanding mood. I wanted to tell her that it was summer, so we didn't have any homework, and I wanted to tell her that I had already made my bed and my room was pretty clean. I wanted to tell her that, but I knew better. Instead, Scottie and Lizzie and I went to our room and got our record player out. We put the player on Scottie's lower bunk, plugged it in, and then got a blanket and tucked it under my mattress so that it hung down to the floor. We also put a blanket at the end of the bed, so inside of the blankets it was really dark. This was one of our favorite things to do. It felt like we were in a completely different world.

Scottie and I had both been given flashlights for Christmas that year, so we climbed into the dark, makeshift fort, and turned on our flashlights. I let Lizzie use mine. Scottie and Lizzie pointed their lights into every corner of our hideout and then they held the flashlights under their chins so that we could see their faces. The shadows caused dark circles to appear under their eyes, and for a second I got a glimpse of what they were going to look like when they were old. I secretly made a quick wish that we would all still be together then.

Scottie had already grabbed a pile of Walt Disney records from underneath his bed. We loved to listen to stories on the record player. We had *101 Dalmatians*, *Mary Poppins*, *Treasure Island*, *20,000 Leagues under the Sea*, *Snow White,* and a few more. I had every word memorized on every record that we owned. Usually there were two stories on each album. Sometimes the stories were longer, and when Side One was done, we'd flip it over to hear the rest of the story. I would close my eyes and say the words out loud along with the characters in the story. I especially liked to talk British with the *Prince and the Pauper*. That would drive Scottie crazy. He'd ask me to stop, and I would, kind of. I would stop saying the words loudly; I would just barely whisper them. He couldn't even hear me, but he would watch my mouth and it would make him so mad that, eventually, he'd end up saying, 'I'm gonna tell Mom'. He was such a baby. But I had learned from experience that my mother always believed what

Scottie told her. Always. It was my fault because I was older, I should know better, I should be a good example to my little brother.

It seemed like I got in trouble every single day of my life and the other kids in my family hardly ever did. The funny thing was, though, on those rare occasions when one of them did get in trouble, I would usually have to sneak into the bathroom and cry. I hated it when someone else was getting a spanking – it would just kill me. I felt bad because I knew so well what it was like to be in their shoes. And so, even as we were getting lost in the wonderful world of Walt Disney, I was hoping that Angela wouldn't get into too much trouble when she got home. But Angela didn't get home.

Finally, even though my parents probably felt a little foolish, they called Lizzie's Uncle Roy. I think it surprised them how seriously he took them. He showed up in his squad car with his partner, and they started asking a million questions. When and where had she last been seen? Who was the last person that she had spoken to? Did she have a boyfriend? How had she been doing in school? Had she mentioned that anyone was angry with her in the last few weeks? Was she a rebellious teen? Would she have been near the woods down the street near the local public schools? And on and on they went.

I was sitting on the arm of the living room couch – which was the same couch that had been my bed until Lizzie had arrived in Seattle – and I was getting kind of angry at those two policemen. What were they asking all of these questions for? Why didn't they just go and find her? Maybe she got off at the wrong bus stop. Maybe she went over to a friend's house. What did they mean 'Is she a rebellious teen?' Suddenly, I didn't really like Lizzie's uncle anymore. I could feel my face growing hot. I clenched my fists together so tightly that my nails left deep, crescent-moon shaped imprints in the flesh of my palms. I wanted them to just go away.

I wanted them to leave, and for Angela to get home and to explain that the cheerleading squad coach had asked her to come to the store with her to buy new pom-poms, and she couldn't say no, of course, because, after all, she was a teacher, and that she had wanted to call, only there just hadn't been time. I wanted to hear something like that because there had to be a simple explanation for why Angela hadn't gotten home at her usual time. There just had to be.

Finally, the questioning seemed to be over, and Uncle Roy asked my dad to come down to the police station with him. After they left, the other kids – who had all been listening from the hallway – came into the living room and slumped onto the couch and the floor. My mom headed straight to the kitchen to pick up where she had left off in her dinner preparations. Normally she would have asked Angela to help her. That night, she didn't seem to want anyone's help.

We all looked at Graham as if to say, 'You're the oldest. What's going on? Where is Angela? What's going to happen?' But Graham was just staring at a pillow that he was holding on his lap, picking lint out from underneath a cloth-covered button. When no one said anything, Graham finally muttered something under his breath.

"What, Graham?" I asked. "What did you say?" I couldn't stand the silence. I wanted someone to talk and make me feel better. Graham gave me a miserable look.

"I should've come right back from Burger King," he confessed. "I should've let Mom know that Angela wasn't at work. If something happens to Angela, it will be all my fault."

"What could happen to Angela?" Scottie asked. We all rolled our eyes like Scottie was a complete idiot, but if we were honest with ourselves, every one of us was probably thinking the same question. What could possibly have happened to Angela? She wouldn't hurt a flea. Who would want to hurt her? Adele started to cry which made me start to cry and then Lizzie too. The boys weren't crying. The only time that I had ever seen the boys cry was when our dog, Sam, got run over by a car, back in Richland. Sam used to chase cars all the time.

"Sam, stop!" I'd yell. "Come here. Sam. SAM!!!" I often came close to throwing my body in front of the car in order to prevent Sam from being crushed by it. But he always seemed to know just how close he could get to that back wheel without getting so close that he ended up underneath it. Graham told me that I was making things worse by chasing him.

"Just let him go, he gets tired soon and he always comes back," he said. "When you chase him it gets him all excited and he just takes longer to tire out." I knew that he was probably right, but if I was ever present when Sam got loose and took off after yet another car, I could not just wait there. I had to run after him. I had to try and save him.

The day that Sam got hit, he was following Graham, who was riding on his bike. Graham was heading to the Big Pool in the middle of town. Every family in the town of Richland belonged to the Big Pool. It cost seventeen dollars a summer for a family of seven. I remember thinking how expensive that was, and how nice my parents were to let us join.

While we were swimming, Sam loved to play on the sprawling lawn around the chain link fence that surrounded the pool. But that day he was following Graham. As he was loping along behind him, Sam caught sight of another dog and veered off the sidewalk. The driver of the car didn't see him until it was too late. Poor Sam. He didn't even die doing what he loved to do best: nipping at the back wheel of a speeding car. He wasn't disobeying anybody. He was just involved in an accident, pure and simple, and it cost him his life. Graham felt like it was all his fault. I could never forget the sight of Graham speeding into the yard on his bike, tears pouring down his face.

"Sam is dead!" he cried. "He got hit by a car." The rest of us kids had been wrapping our towels around our necks and getting ready to bike over to the pool. As Graham leaned against the car, sobbing, we all dropped our bikes and stood there, staring at our big brother, who we didn't even recognize.

My mom came out of the house and listened as Graham explained to her what had just happened. She was strangely calm. She told Graham to go get a big box from the basement, and she went and got the keys to our brown Chevy station wagon. We all piled into the car without being told to do so, and Graham came back out with the flattened box. We put the seats down so that the entire back of the interior of the car was open, and I sat in a circle with my brothers and sisters, trying really hard not to make eye contact with any of them, but I knew that everyone of us was crying.

When we got to the place where Sam laid lifeless on the side of the road, my mom pulled the car over to the curb. We gathered around our beloved Sam. By this time, we weren't even ashamed of our tears – we were bawling loudly. Graham bent down and lifted him up. He looked like he was asleep, except his little tongue was hanging out of his mouth and there was blood on it. Graham placed Sam ever so gently into the box that he had opened up, and then we carried the box like pallbearers and slid it into the back of the wagon. There was hardly enough room to get back into the car, but we all squished in, and my mom took us home.

She must have called my dad first thing, because he caught the bus and got home not much after we did. He started crying, too, when he saw Sam lying dead in the box. It was a horrible, horrible day. We buried Sam right there in the yard. Scottie and I made a little wooden cross and stuck it in the ground later that night.

Even though I was so sad that I felt sick to my stomach, I also felt really bad for Graham that day. I knew that he was blaming himself. I knew, even though I wished that he had been more careful (or that he had tied Sam up that day and not let him follow him to the pool), that it wasn't his fault. It really wasn't anybody's fault, not even Sam's. It was just an accident – it was just an accident.

And there we were, everyone except Angela, and once again Graham was blaming himself for the bad thing that was happening to us that day. At that point I think we were all really glad that there hadn't been an accident, like with Sam, but as the weeks went by, it seemed like we were all beginning to find ourselves wishing that there *had* just been an accident. The unknown was much, much worse.

Those first few days that Angela was missing all seemed like a blur. There were policemen and phone calls and neighbors dropping in, and dozens and dozens of church friends and well-wishers. I was amazed at all the people who showed up; most of them brought Tupperware containers full of food. There were tuna fish casseroles and carrot and raisin salads and someone even brought my favorite Jell-O dish with the marshmallows. Somewhere in the back of my mind I wondered if my disappearance would have created such a stir, but then the very real fact that my sister was missing would hit me and I would begin to feel hollow again.

Where was she? Why didn't she just come home? I thought of all the times that I had gotten mad at her for beating me at Spit, and I felt so awful. If I could just have my old life back again – if I could just have one more chance – I would show Angela how much I loved her. I would never cry, even if she beat me every time.

We kids figured out quickly that it was in our best interest to stay very far away from our mother. At first, I stayed very close to her, waiting for her to smile and give me the good news that all was well, but my hovering made her nervous. She turned to me at one point and told me to go to my room, and I knew, by the look in her eyes, that she was actually saying 'Can't you see that I don't know? Can't you see that I'm scared to death?' I realized then that my mother was in no state to comfort anybody – she just didn't have it in her. So I took it upon myself to take care of Scottie and Lizzie. They needed to be protected.

At first, I wanted to distract them. But then it occurred to me that maybe we could actually help. Scottie and Lizzie and I were practically sleuths already. What other ten- and eight-year-olds had read almost every single one of the *Hardy Boys* adventures? If we weren't capable of solving a mystery, then I didn't know who was. We started out by meeting in the tree house in the back yard. First, we had to see if we had any clues. I looked at Scottie, and Scottie looked at Lizzie and Lizzie looked at me. We didn't know where to start, so we decided to go over what the police were worried about. They thought that Angela might be a rebellious teen. We knew that wasn't true. They thought that maybe she had an enemy. We knew that Angela was loved by everybody. They wondered if Angela had been by the woods near the elementary school. Had she? Yes, it was very possible that Angela had been by the woods by the school – because that would have been the normal way she walked to get to the Burger King. But, she hadn't been scheduled to work that day. Maybe she had been asked to work at the last minute. I wondered if her uniform was gone. Had anyone even looked to see if Angela had changed into her Burger King uniform?

I told Scottie and Lizzie to stay there, and that I would be right back. I climbed down the tree and ran to Angela's room. I knew where Angela kept her uniform; I loved to look through Angela's dresser drawers. She had the best clothes ever. I remember overhearing a conversation between Michelle and Theresa, Angela's girlfriends. Michelle said that she thought Angela had the grooviest clothes of anyone she knew. I felt the same way. I loved to touch her shiny, polyester blouses, and try on her soft, velvet chokers. I'm sure she would not have been thrilled if she had known that I would occasionally sneak into her room to look at her stuff, but I really couldn't help myself. I didn't do it all that often, because she and Adele were constantly in her room those days whispering about boys or whatever – but every now and then, when they were nowhere around, I would slip into their teenage world.

It turns out that maybe it was a good thing I was a snoop. Who else would have known where to look for her uniform? It was always in the second drawer down on the left hand side of her dresser. I pulled the drawer open, and – ah hah! – it was not there. Angela's Burger King uniform was not in her drawer. That meant that she *had* gone to work that afternoon. My mom must have been talking with Nicky's mom when Angela got home from cheerleading practice that day, and Angela must have gotten a call, changed, and headed off to work. That had to be it.

Lizzie and Scottie and I had spent most of the afternoon of June third in Nicky's back yard because it had been raining all day the day before, and we were dying to get outside and play. Nicky's dad, Mr. Anderson, had been in the back yard with us. He had come home from lunch with a tire swing for Nicky, and he was hooking it up to their biggest tree as we stood around and watched. After Mr. Anderson went back to work, my mom and Nicky's mom sat on the steps and talked while the four of us played in the back yard. Mom must have left at some point to start dinner or clean the house or something while we were playing. We were too busy to notice. Even though he was much younger than we were, we liked playing at Nicky's house. He was an only child and had the best toys in the neighborhood – plus, Mrs. Anderson would sometimes bring out popsicles or ice cream bars if we played with him long enough. The only reason we even left when we did that afternoon was because of the fire. Once the Haunted Mansion started burning, we all stopped what we were doing.

"Okay, Guys," I said, after climbing back up into the tree house. "Angela's uniform is gone. They must have needed her at work. They probably called just after she got home." Lizzie and Scottie nodded their heads in agreement.

"Are you writing this down, Scottie?" I asked him. Earlier, I had given him the notebook that I kept in the secret box in our tree house.

"What am I supposed to be writing?" Scottie asked me. I looked at the page in the notebook. He hadn't written down one word I said. Instead, he was drawing peace signs, smiley faces and the peering eyes and nose of Kilroy all over the page.

"Scottie, come on! This is really important!" I grabbed the notebook, and showed Lizzie his artwork. Lizzie giggled into her hand. "Lizzie!" I said, shaking my head, but then I started laughing, too.

"Okay – fine," I said, trying to look serious, "it looks like I'll just have to do this myself." I started to write down my thoughts: 'uniform gone' and 'Angela went to work' and 'Angela walked by woods'...

"I wonder why they took note of that?" I said, thinking out loud. "What do you think? Have we even figured out why the police were wondering if Angela had been by those woods?"

Lizzie sat up on her knees. "You know, I was wondering about that, too," she said. "Aren't those the woods that you took me to ride in on my first day here, Bobbi?"

Scottie let out a gasp. "Bobbi! You took Lizzie to the forbidden woods? If Mom knew, she would kill you."

I quickly put my hand over Scottie's mouth, pushing him against the side of the tree. "Shhh – Scottie, shut up!" Scottie's eyes grew bigger and I knew he was thinking, 'If Mom heard you say shut up she would kill you'.

"Why do you call them the forbidden woods?" Lizzie asked.

"Because," Scottie replied, "girls get their clothes taken off in those woods."

Lizzie looked at me with surprise in her eyes. "You took me into a forest where girls get their clothes taken off?" she asked.

"Well, yeah," I admitted. "Scottie and I found some clothes in those woods, and it kind of creeped us out. But the best trails in Seattle are in those woods."

"We used to take a shortcut through there on the way home," Scottie said. "But our parents told us we weren't allowed to anymore on account of the missing girls."

"The missing girls?" Lizzie exclaimed. I could tell that she was getting really scared and probably a little mad at me for risking her life on her first day in Seattle.

"Scottie, we don't know that there were any girls missing. Just girls missing their clothes," I said. He could be so irritating sometimes.

"Then why did Mom and Dad tell us we couldn't take the shortcut anymore, huh?" I hated to admit it, but Scottie made a good point. When our parents had forbidden us to take the shortcut home from school, we had felt sure that the reason was that someone, maybe lots of people, had been found dead in those woods. Why had I taken Lizzie there? Suddenly, I wasn't sure. All I knew was that I wanted Lizzie to have fun, and those woods did have the best trails.

We needed to go back there, but not for fun. If we knew that Angela had been by the woods – and we knew that the policemen had specifically asked if she'd been there – then those woods probably held our first clue. I checked my watch. It was one in the afternoon. Angela had been missing for more than two and a half days. Our house was full of policemen and well-meaning friends, but it seemed to us that no one was actually doing anything. Lizzie and Scottie and I climbed down from our tree and went to the basement where our garage was. There were two doors and they opened outward, not up. Scottie and I each grabbed the handle of one of the doors and started to pull on them. They were really heavy and the metal drop bolts screeched as we dragged them across the concrete. The noise made me remember something that had happened a few days after we moved to Seattle, in the middle of the night.

My dad had been studying in our room when he heard a noise. Scottie and I were dead asleep; it was before my insomnia had set in. The noise was so strange that my dad got up from his calculus and quietly crossed the room and opened the door. Our bedroom door actually opened up onto a tiny covered porch. You had to open another exterior door in order to get into the big part of the house, and that door creaked and groaned when you opened it. The noise that my dad made sneaking out of our room jolted me awake. I lay there for a while, wondering why he had left the light on. Usually, when he was done studying, he would turn off the light and go to bed. Clearly, he wasn't done studying, so what was he doing? My curiosity got the better of me and I climbed out of bed and made my way into the big house. As I was shutting the kitchen door, I saw my dad coming out of the hallway with a flashlight in his hand.

"What are you doing, Daddy?" I asked.

He put his finger to his mouth. "Shhh," he whispered, "I think someone is in our basement." I'm sure my eyes looked like they were going to pop out of my head.

"Can I come with you?" I whispered back.

"No. Go get your mother" my dad replied, and then he opened the door to the basement and disappeared down the stairs. I was afraid that I would miss all the action if I went to get my mother on the other side of the house, so I waited for a second, and then followed my dad down the stairs. There, standing in our basement, holding onto our Honda 50's, were two boys. A third boy was pushing on one of the heavy garage doors. It screeched loudly and then got stuck. He could not get it open wide enough to get the motorcycles out.

"What do you boys think you are doing?" my dad yelled. The three boys completely panicked. If it hadn't been so terrible, it would have been funny. The two who were holding the 50's threw the bikes over, and made for the door. My dad was angry and he started to run after them. And so did I – how dare they touch our mini bikes? Two of the boys got away, but my dad grabbed the third one.

"Way to go, Dad!" I screamed.

He looked up at me. "Where is your mother?" he asked as he wrestled the squirming boy to the ground.

"Oops, I forgot," I said, and started yelling, "Mommy, Mommy! Daddy caught a burglar!" By this time my dad was sitting on the kid, pinning him to the floor of the basement.

"Stop screaming, Bobbi, and go and get her," he said calmly. "Quietly." I quickly ran upstairs and up to my mom's room and threw myself onto my parents' bed. My mother screamed and sat up in bed like *I* was a burglar or something.

"Mom, it's me, Bobbi," I said.

She blinked at me in a dazed way. "Bobbi, what in the world is wrong with you?" My mom was so mad!

"Daddy is sitting on a burglar right now, Mom. He's in the basement." She could not have looked more confused but, at my insistence, she got out of bed, grabbed her robe and followed me down the stairs. She actually looked surprised to see my dad downstairs sitting on the strange teenage kid. What, did she think I had made it up?

"Daddy!" she exclaimed, "what in heaven's name is going on here?"

My dad looked up at her. "I caught this young man trying to get away with one of our Honda 50's. Two other boys got away." My mom looked like she might faint, so I went and put my arm around her waist.

"Well, what are you going to do with him?" my mom asked.

"I don't know," Daddy replied, "I'm just not sure." My dad was too nice. I was thinking that we should throw the kid in jail – how dare he try to steal our stuff? Especially our Hondas! But my dad, I could tell, was not really interested in getting the boy in trouble with the law. The boy, I was pretty sure, was in for a lecture.

"Sit up, Young Man," he said. So the boy sat up, and started to wipe the dirt off his clothes. "Do you know the seriousness of what you attempted to do tonight?" he asked him earnestly. The boy just stared at his feet. "Look at me when I talk to you," my dad said sternly. I watched the boy's face. I think he would rather have been turned over to the police than to have to look my dad in the eye. But Daddy wasn't going anywhere. He found two chairs for them, and they sat and talked in the basement for at least an hour. I was amazed to see the boy cry as he told my dad how sorry he was. It turns out he didn't have a dad and his mom worked a day job and nights as a waitress. He was out of control, and he knew it. He was real sorry, and he promised never to do it again.

My dad got the boy to write down his address and phone number, and he told him that he was going to pick him up on Sunday and take him to church with us. And he did just that. The kid's name was Hank, and a year later he was still coming with us every Sunday to church.

I was kind of irritated with my dad that night for befriending the enemy, but I have to admit, Hank turned out to be a really sweet kid. I think Daddy probably saved his life that night and, I don't know, he may have even saved his everlasting soul.

We got the doors opened, finally, and went straight over to our red and yellow Hondas. Our plan was to push the bikes until we got far enough away from our parents – or any of the other adults roaming around our house – so that they would not hear the engines when we started the bikes.

Lizzie rode with me on the yellow Honda, wearing one of the helmets. Scottie rode the red mini bike and wore the other helmet. We only had two helmets, and I felt like the younger kids should wear them. I would just be real careful. Once we were three blocks away, we started the engines. We decided that we would drive all along Highland Terrace Drive from one end of the woods to the other before we even went into the forest. I told Scottie to start on the edge of the woods closest to our house; Lizzie and I would ride to the other edge and come toward our house. We would meet somewhere in the middle and discuss what we found. So, Lizzie and I sped away. I was gunning it, because I was anxious to start looking for signs of Angela. Once Lizzie and I reached the end of the woods, we turned around and started our search. Inch by inch, we made our way over the shoulder of the road. We were looking for – what? Signs of a tussle? Angela's Burger King hat? Something that might have fallen out of her purse? We weren't even sure what it was that we were looking for, but we knew that if it was there, we would find it.

When Scottie and Lizzie and I met halfway on Highland Terrace Drive, not one of us had seen anything but a couple of empty Rainier beer cans and some trash that people had flung from their cars. There was nothing that made us think that Angela had been walking there recently, nothing at all.

"Should we go into the woods, or do you think that maybe we should double-check the shoulder of the road?" I asked. It wasn't that I didn't trust Scottie, but there was something in me that just wanted to be sure that he hadn't gotten distracted for even a moment. "Why don't we do that, huh?" I said, answering my own question. "You make sure that Lizzie and I didn't miss anything, and we'll go over the ground that you covered."

"Okay – whatever you say," Scottie replied. I was surprised that he was taking my orders so easily. I think he was finally beginning to understand what could have actually happened to

Angela. Lizzie and I started off from the center of the woods, heading toward our house. We went slowly. The engine kept stalling on our mini bike, but each time I just started it back up and we kept on looking. We came to a place where it looked like a vehicle had pulled off the road onto the shoulder. There were deep ruts where it had obviously gotten stuck in the mud. I stopped the mini bike there and we sat still for a minute.

"What do you think, Lizzie?" I asked her.

"I think we should get off here," she replied, "and take a closer look." I nodded and we both swung our legs off the bike. Lizzie started walking over the hardened ruts, while I leaned the bike on a tree.

"Bobbi, come here!" I heard her say, and I ran over to where Lizzie was crouching. "Look," she said. She was pointing to something bright that was squished deep into a tire tread. It looked like a ribbon. I grabbed one end and carefully pulled it out of the dried mud. Sure enough, it was a purple ribbon. I wanted to get excited and to think that we had found a clue – Angela definitely had purple ribbons – but then it occurred to me that Angela was wearing a red, gold, and blue uniform. She would never be caught dead wearing a purple ribbon with those colors.

Caught dead – I cringed at the thought. Since Angela had disappeared, I had begun to notice how many common phrases there were that referred to death: 'Over my dead body'; 'It about killed me'; 'I'd rather die'... I used to use those expressions all the time, but now they bothered me.

Even though I knew the ribbon couldn't have been Angela's, I didn't want to make Lizzie feel bad, so I tucked it in my pocket. We got back on the mini bike and kept on looking. We didn't find anything, and neither did Scottie. I felt discouraged, and I could tell that Scottie and Lizzie were feeling ready to give up, too. Of course, we knew better than to expect that we could solve the mystery in a day, but we had really hoped that maybe we would have discovered some teeny little clue that would explain what had happened to our sister, and where we should look next. But we hadn't turned up anything.

Scottie and Lizzie and I regrouped again. We decided that we had no choice but to look inside the forbidden woods. Unlike the last time I had taken Lizzie there, this time we did not feel like exploring. It was starting to get dark, and we were scared. But we knew how important it was, so we faced our fears. We rode through the forest that late evening, looking and looking for, again, we weren't sure what; Angela, I guess. But Angela was not there, and after an hour of riding over trails that had, in a previous life, given us much pleasure, we gave up. We rode home; all the way home, not even caring if our parents heard us puttering into the back yard on our motorbikes.

13

When we got inside the house, Adele saw us and followed us into our room. She climbed up onto my top bunk. It wasn't often that Adele came into our room. Lizzie, Scottie, and I weren't really sure what to say. We didn't end up having to say anything because Adele started talking.

"I just miss her so much, You Guys. Everything reminds me of her. I smell her perfume all over this house. I keep feeling like I'm going to scream, and then I stop myself and start to pray. I pray and I pray, and then I – I start to feel crazy, like I, well, you know, like I should be doing something. But what am I supposed to be doing?"

Adele had been trying to hold back her tears, but now she burst out crying. I started crying too; I couldn't help myself. I wanted to crawl up onto my bunk next to my sister and put my arms around her, but I felt embarrassed and awkward, and so I just stood there, looking at my feet, letting the tears run down my face and plop onto the floor.

"I uh, was, uh, home when she, uh, got home, from cheerleading practice," Adele stammered. She was having difficulty getting her words out around her sobs. I looked up at her, wanting to hear what she was trying to say. Adele's face was as red as her hair.

"You were home?" I asked her, as I wiped my nose with the back of my hand. Adele took a deep breath before she answered.

"Yeah, but I barely even talked to her," she explained, "because it was my day for blackberries and I needed to get outside. I had been reading all day and didn't realize how late it was. When Angela got home, I just barely said 'hi' to her on my way out the door."

We had every imaginable fruit growing in our yard: apple trees, apricot trees, peach trees, plum trees and blackberry bushes that went on forever. One of our standard chores was to go out back and pick a bucket of fruit for Mom. That day it had been Adele's turn.

"Adele," I said, "did you talk to her at all? Did she tell you what she was going to do later on that day?"

"Yeah," she replied. "She got home and then the phone rang. They wanted to know if she could work."

"Really? Did she say yes?" I asked. Adele nodded. "She was supposed to be there by four."

"Did you talk to Lizzie's uncle about this? Does he know that she went to work that afternoon?" Adele just looked at me as if she hadn't heard me. She let out a deep breath as she closed her eyes.

"The last time I saw her, she was putting on her uniform and looking for her ribbons."

"What color ribbons?" I demanded, and I scrambled onto the top bunk next to her.

"Bobbi, calm down! Why are you asking me all these questions?" Adele asked. Her face was getting even redder, if that was possible.

"I'm just wondering," I replied. "Was she wearing ribbons when she left?" Adele just shrugged her shoulders.

"I can't remember – I was afraid that Mom would walk in and find out that I hadn't even started to pick the blackberries yet," she confessed.

"Think carefully, Adele," I urged her. "What color ribbons were in her hair when she got home from practice?" Adele wrinkled her brow as she tried to think back.

"Bobbi, I don't know. All I'm saying is that I feel horrible that the last time I ever saw Angela, I barely said 'hi'."

"Adele," I said forcefully, "you are going to see Angela again. You've got to believe that." She moved to the edge of the bed and slid to the floor.

"I hope you're right, Bobbi," she said. And then she left our room.

"We have to get your uncle, Lizzie," I said quickly. "We have to tell him everything that Adele just told us."

"What did she say that was so important?" Scottie asked. I looked at him and didn't say anything. As Adele had been talking, I envisioned Angela coming home from practice in her purple and gold cheerleading outfit. I pulled the purple ribbon from my pocket and wondered...

14

I could tell that Uncle Roy was exasperated with Adele when he found out that she had spoken with Angela on the day of her disappearance and hadn't told him. Adele felt terrible.

"You never asked," she said defensively. And she was right – he hadn't asked. He'd talked to the adults, but he'd never once stopped and asked us kids anything. He must have realized his mistake, because after he got every bit of information out of Adele, he turned to interrogate me.

"Now, then, where exactly did you find this ribbon?" he asked me. "Can you take me there right now?"

"Yes, Sir," I said, and headed for the basement. Uncle Roy caught my arm.

"Whoa," he said, "where do you think you're going?"

"I'm going to get my Honda 50," I replied, looking at him impatiently.

He laughed. "Why don't we just take my squad car, huh?"

I turned and faced him. "Really?" I asked. "Can Lizzie and Scottie come too?"

Uncle Roy looked at his watch. "You've got two minutes to get them." I ran to the tree house as fast as I could, calling out their names.

The four of us drove to the spot on Highland Terrace Drive where Lizzie had found the ribbon. I told Uncle Roy where to stop the car, but he parked it farther down the road so that he wouldn't roll over the tire prints. I respected him for that. I showed him where the ribbon had been stuck in one of the ruts. Uncle Roy immediately called for another officer to come to the scene in order to make molds of the tire treads. While we were waiting for the other policeman to get there, I walked around the tire prints, looking to see if there was anything else that would give me a hint that Angela might have been there. The area was uneven and hard to walk on. It was Scottie who found the footprints.

"Bobbi," he observed, "these could be Angela's footprints, couldn't they?" And sure enough, there, between some tire tracks, were the imprints of a girl's shoe. I noticed how small they were.

Even though Angela was sixteen, she still had a size six shoe. Everything about Angela was petite.

"Scottie, you're brilliant. Why didn't I see these before?" I called out to Uncle Roy, who was talking on his radio in the car. I showed him the prints that Scottie had come upon. Uncle Roy scratched his chin and stared at the small prints.

"Would you look at that?" Uncle Roy exclaimed. He wasn't really talking to us, but we were listening to what he was saying. When he realized that he had an audience, he pointed to the ground.

"Do you see the larger prints surrounding these smaller prints?" he asked us. At first I couldn't see them, but when I stood back a bit, I could see – between the tire treads and the deep ruts – a number of big footprints tracked all over the same area.

"This is good, isn't it?" I asked Uncle Roy. "I mean, these are real clues, right?" He stood there nodding his head and scratching his chin, and it seemed to me like he was saying, 'Yeah, this is good'.

15

Life is kind of strange. In the middle of my family's crisis, the rest of the world carried on like nothing at all had changed. People turned on the radio to find out what the weather would be like, they showered, and went to work, and ate their sandwiches for lunch. And even we Johnsons had returned to a semi-normal routine. I felt guilty for going on with my life like nothing was wrong, and yet, what choice do the living really have? Not that I thought of Angela as being among the non-living. No, no – I just thought of her as being in limbo. I could not let myself think that anything bad was happening to her. In my mind, she was just lost, and we were in the process of helping her find her way home.

We had been invited to go over to a friend's house for dinner one Sunday after Angela had disappeared. My parents decided that maybe it was a good idea for all of us to do something other than worry about Angela, so they said that we would be happy to come over for dinner after church. They lived in Kent, which was out in the country, and they encouraged us to bring our mini bikes so that we kids would have something to do after dinner while the adults talked.

The meal was a strained event. The food was good, but everyone was just thinking about Angela. No one wanted to bring up the stressful topic, and yet it seemed disrespectful to talk about anything else, so there was very little talk over dinner. The sound of utensils clinking and the occasional 'please pass the salt' were the only noises that broke the silence. I was never so happy to be dismissed from a dinner table.

"You kids go on and ride your mini bikes, but don't go too far!" my parents warned us. Scottie and Lizzie and I promised that we wouldn't, and we were out of there. Lizzie and I were still wearing our church clothes. Lizzie was wearing a pink dress with white anklets and I was wearing a white and yellow gingham dress with brand-new white polyester knee socks. Even as we were tearing off the property on our mini bikes, all I kept thinking was that we'd better be very careful not to get our Sunday clothes messed up, or Mom would kill us.

We were so far out in the county that the roads weren't even paved. The freedom was exhilarating. Lizzie and I were ahead of Scottie, so I kept looking back every once in a while to make sure that he was still with us. The road took a sharp right, and we followed it only to discover that it now paralleled two sets of railroad tracks. Scottie came up next to us.

"I wonder if trains still go on those tracks?" he yelled.

"It doesn't look like it," I yelled back. "There are a lot of weeds growing up around the tracks." He agreed and we rode on for a distance. After a bit, we came to a place where the road was even with the tracks, almost like it was a crossing, but the only thing on the other side of the tracks was a dense forest. Scottie came to a stop right there on the flat area.

"Want to cross over into the woods?" he asked. I looked at Lizzie and she shrugged, which I took to be a yes.

"Sure," I said. "Let's go!" Scottie took the lead; we bumped right along behind him and soon we were in the shade of the forest, riding on soft, sweet-smelling pine needles. They cushioned the ride, but you had to be very careful on the turns because they were slippery.

"Good idea, Scottie!" I remarked. It was nice and cool in the woods, and it looked like someone had been there before us either on motorcycles or on horses, because there was a pretty wide path leading into the forest that looked very inviting. We rode along a little more slowly once we were in the woods. When we came to a hill, Lizzie and I could only get up halfway. We started to slip on the pine needles and it felt like the bike might end up falling over on us, so I turned into the slide and rode back down the hill. Scottie made it all the way up and he looked put out that we were still at the bottom of the hill.

"What're you waiting for?" he shouted. "Come on up." We tried again. I revved the little engine and maneuvered my way up the hill only to get about halfway up and to again feel the bottom giving out on us one more time. I turned back into the slide and coasted back to the bottom of the hill.

"I don't think we can make it, Scottie," I called up to him. He threw his head back in disgust.

"Just push it up!" he yelled back. I really didn't want to, but I also didn't want Scottie to be able to say that I couldn't do something he could.

"Okay. We'll give it a try," I said. I revved the engine just enough to help me get the bike up the hill. Lizzie, in the meantime, was trying to climb up the hill next to me, but she kept slipping and sliding in her slick Mary Janes. I was weaving to the right and to the left. Pine needles were shooting everywhere as I tried to keep hold of the mini bike. We were only a little ways up the hill and we were already exhausted.

"How did you get up there?" I screamed to Scottie. I was mad. This was so stupid. Scottie was sitting on his mini bike, revving the engine impatiently.

"Come on, You Guys," he said. "It's easy."

"Forget it, Scottie. We can't do it," I said in frustration. "Are you okay, Lizzie?" I asked as I headed back down the hill.

"Yeah," she said, "I need my tennis shoes, though." She and I were both wearing our patent leather Sunday shoes – if Scottie made fun of us later, I would be able to blame it on them. Scottie rode back down and kept going, so Lizzie and I jumped on our mini bike and took off after him. He headed out of the woods, back to the railroad tracks. He only stopped when we finally pulled up next to him.

"What do you think?" he asked. "Do you want to cross back over?" To be honest, I was really tired out by that time, and I was pretty sure that Lizzie was, too, but she would never complain.

"Yeah, let's go back," I said. Scottie nodded and we all made our way over to the railroad tracks. The rails were on a slope at that spot and were harder to get over than they had been where we had crossed before. I pushed the mini bike over the first set of tracks, went down the hill, and then pushed it back up the hill to do it again over the next two rails. Once we were on the other side of the tracks, Lizzie and I went up to the shoulder of the dirt road and stopped. I leaned the bike on a rickety fence and then we carefully sat down on some grass, trying not to get dirty. Scottie was still standing by the first set of tracks. It appeared that he had not been as successful as I had been at getting his mini bike over the first rail.

"What's the matter, Scottie?" I yelled out to him.

"I don't know," he muttered. "Something got stuck on this dumb rail." Lizzie and I sat there and watched as he tried to lift the back of his bike over the rail. It didn't budge. Scottie heaved at it with a grunt, but it wouldn't come loose. I was sitting there thinking that I would have to go help him, when out of the clear blue sky we all heard the loud WHOOOOOOO! Lizzie and I both jumped up and stared in the direction that the noise was coming from. Scottie instinctively started to pull harder on the handlebars.

"Scottie – it's a train!" Lizzie and I both screamed at the same time. We heard the train, and worse, we could see the train. It wasn't more than maybe two football fields away, and it was coming down the same tracks on which Scottie's bike was stuck. My first thought was to desert the bike and make a run for it, but then, somewhere in the back of my brain, I wondered what would happen if the train hit the mini bike. Would it buckle and end up taking us out in its wake?

"Take the bike and go," I told Lizzie. "Get away from here now!" And then I ran up and over to Scottie and pushed him out of the way. I grabbed the back of the bike and started yanking on it with all my might. The words 'fight like your life depended on it' were running through my brain, and on some level I remember thinking, actually, my life probably did depend on it. I felt a strange urge to start laughing. Scottie stood up, grabbed the back wheel, and started pulling, too.

"Jesus, please help us!" I screamed. But the train just got closer and closer. It might seem like an exaggeration to say this, but amazingly, just in the nick of time, something released on the bike, and with one last yank, we sent it flying over the rail. It tumbled down the embankment and we tumbled after it. We were so close to the train's engine that, as it bore down on us and then rumbled past us in a rush, we could see the look of panic and anger on the engineer's face, and the angry fist that he was shaking at us. Scottie and I just lay there until every last car passed us by. After the caboose had been gone for a good minute, Scottie let out a sigh.

"I guess trains *do* still go on these tracks," he said flatly. I just closed my eyes and started to laugh.

Lizzie had obeyed me and had driven the yellow Honda 50 as fast as she could away from the disaster waiting to happen. She had it in her mind that she was going to get our parents. But when she didn't hear a crash, and she could tell that the train was long gone, she turned back around to see what had happened to us. Scottie and I were still lying in the weeds between the two tracks when she got back.

"Are you okay?" she called out uncertainly.

"Yeah, we're okay, Lizzie," I yelled out to her. "We'll be right there." I turned my head to look at Scottie. He was lying flat on his back, looking straight up in the sky. I do believe that he was asking God to forgive him for every bad thing that he had ever done for as long as he had lived.

"I guess we'd better get out of here, huh?" I said to him.

"Yeah," he said, "I guess." He grabbed his bike and pushed it up the next incline, only this time he was very careful to lift the bike up and over the rail. He did it with no problem.

We were never sure what part of the mini bike got stuck on that train track. Scottie later told me that he thought it was God's way of letting him know that, even when things looked really bad, He was always watching out for him. "Or," he said, "He might have been telling us to stop taking such stupid chances."

It was an enormous relief to be back on the straight dirt road after our frightening experience. Once again, Lizzie and I got ahead of Scottie, and I had to keep looking back to make sure that he was still following us. One of those times that I was looking back, we came to the sharp curve where the road took a turn – I had not seen it coming. The next thing I knew, I was plowing headlong into a split-rail fence. Thankfully, the fence was old and decaying, so it splintered into a thousand, soft, mulchy pieces, sending millions of little white bugs everywhere. I fell over with the bike, and Lizzie was thrown on to the wet, grassy earth. She jumped up and started to shake the bugs and dirt off of her body and out of her hair. The bike ended up on top of my leg, and the boiling hot engine manifold pressed directly on my right calf. It burned deep into my skin and – even worse – it burned a hole right through my brand-new white polyester sock. I started to scream and Lizzie quickly came over and pulled the mini bike off of me.

"Quick, Bobbi," she screamed. "You're covered with bugs!" I momentarily forgot my pain and desperately started to shake myself off.

"Are they gone?" I asked. Lizzie was knocking them off my back as I shook my head upside down. When we were both certain that we'd gotten the tiny white worms off, I remembered the burn on my inner calf. All I could think of, as I pulled the smoking sock down around my ankle, and the smell of my own scorched flesh reached my nostrils, was 'Mom is going to kill me'.

When we got back to the house where my parents were still visiting with their friends, I quickly switched socks. I put the good sock on my right foot and the burnt one on my left foot, and then rolled it down to hide the hole from my mother. Lizzie and I sneaked into the bathroom and watered down some Kleenex. We then carefully flattened it out on my burn. It was all I could do not to scream from the pain. But there was no way that I was going to let my mom know what had happened. So I placed the wad of wet tissue on my burn and ever so carefully pulled the white knee sock over the top of it so that it was held securely. That night, when we got home, I bunched both socks up and shoved them into the bottom of the kitchen garbage pail.

Thankfully, my mother never discovered the missing socks. I guess she had a few more important things on her mind at the time. She didn't even notice me favoring my leg for the next three or four weeks. It seemed like that burn was never going to get better. I had to wear knee socks the whole summer long in order to hide it. It finally healed, but the pinkish scar on the inner side of my right calf never went away.

16

Uncle Roy put the ribbon that we found in a manila envelope with the word "Evidence" printed on it in bold black letters. He and the other officer also made molds of the tire tracks and the footprints. In spite of ourselves, we were fascinated by what the police were doing. They seemed to have forgotten that we were still there because they talked to each other openly about their thoughts on the case.

"What do you think, Roy? Any similarities between this girl and that student nurse at Harborview who disappeared a month ago?"

"You know," Uncle Roy replied, "that's the first thing I thought of when I got this call, but to be honest with you, there really aren't any significant similarities. She was a college girl, for one thing."

"Yeah, I know, I thought of that," he said. "She was twenty-one years old, living on her own somewhere on First Hill. This girl is only sixteen, and living at home. These two cases don't really seem to be related, do they?" Uncle Roy scratched his chin again and shook his head. "I just don't know. There's not enough information to make a connection or rule one out."

"What's the latest on that student nurse?" the detective asked.

Uncle Roy sighed. "I hate to tell you, but things have kind of gone cold," he said. "The problem is, no one knew that she was missing for two days. Makes it hard."

His colleague nodded. "Maybe she decided to visit an aunt in Missouri or something," he suggested.

Uncle Roy let out a deep breath, and I could tell that he was troubled. It clearly bothered him that there were two young girls that he knew about who had gone missing. I wanted to pat his back, to say something encouraging, but I didn't dare. For the first time since Angela had disappeared, I felt a little bit of hope. If policemen like Uncle Roy were on her case, then surely she would be found. The two men finished up what they needed to do, and then they suddenly seemed to become aware of our presence.

"Hey, kids. We need to be getting you home," Uncle Roy said as he wrapped his arm around Lizzie and gave her a squeeze.

"Awww, we're not in any hurry to get home," I said. I was secretly hoping that he would take us downtown to police headquarters.

"Well, I'm sure your mother is making you a big dinner right about now," he said. "I would hate for all that food to go to waste."

"Why don't you eat with us?" I offered. I felt warmly toward Uncle Roy at that moment, and I didn't want him to just drop us off and leave. "I know that my mom would love to hear that you found all of these clues, and she always makes a lot of food."

He gave me a big smile. "I need to be taking these prints down to headquarters," he said, "so that we can figure out who they belong to." Oh, right. What was I thinking? He needed to hurry up and get downtown so that he could figure out who had taken my sister away from us. I felt my face heating up and I knew it was getting red. I hoped that it wasn't noticeable.

"Thanks for the invite," Uncle Roy said. "I promise I will eat with you and your family sometime soon." And then he smiled again.

I couldn't help myself – wrong as I knew it was to be feeling anything but worry and concern over my sister, I think I fell in love with Uncle Roy at that moment. He was my hero. And so, I very willingly allowed him to drop us off at home so that he could get back to the business of saving my sister.

17

It's odd – you would think that if a mother lost one of her children, she would be extra careful not to lose any more. But after Angela went missing, the rest of us were pretty much on our own. Our mother was so distracted by Angela's absence that we could have stayed out all night and I really don't think that she would have noticed. It's not that our mom felt less love for her remaining children. Our mother loved all of us every bit as much as she loved Angela; it's just that her universe had been drastically altered, and she simply didn't know how to proceed. The good thing was that she had done a really good job of loving us before the tragedy occurred. She had purposely, sacrificially given of herself from the moment that she looked upon our newborn faces until the moment that Angela had been taken from us. We knew, even in the midst of our terrible ordeal, that we were still incredibly special to her. We remaining kids made a pact with each other that we would not do anything that would add more stress to our dear mother's life.

It was coming up on Adele's twelfth birthday and, before Angela disappeared, Adele told all of her really good friends that they were invited to her party. After she realized that Angela was probably not going to get back before her birthday, Adele said that she didn't really need a birthday party that year. She was twelve, after all, and really, wasn't that too old to be having a birthday party?

I overheard my parents talking in the kitchen one night after they thought that everyone had gone to bed. My dad said that we couldn't let Adele's birthday go by without celebrating it – it just wouldn't be fair to her. So he suggested to my mom that we do something special for her. He wanted to invite all of Adele's friends to a sleepover on the beach. My dad had recently bought a Coleman pop-up trailer from one of his friends at church, and he and Adele had already talked about having a sleepover party before Angela disappeared. I was sure that my mom was not really up to camping out with a bunch of girls, as anxious as she was, but she was big on making birthdays special for her kids, and she always wanted to make my dad happy. I think she knew that an outing would be good for him, so when he suggested the trip, she said yes. Adele was ecstatic and gleefully told all of her friends. She was not only going to be having a sleepover party, it was going to be on the beach! Adele's friends were excited, and all of us were happy, too. What a relief it was to be able to look forward to doing something fun.

Scottie and Lizzie and I had been spending most of our time trying to find Angela, and we discovered that solving mysteries was harder than we thought. How had Frank and Joe solved forty-nine mysteries (and I heard that their newest mystery, *Danger on Vampire Trail,* was going to be out by the end of the summer)? I guess we were figuring out the difference between real life and fiction. It was easier for me to think of this situation as a mystery, something that could be solved with diligence and hard work, than to dwell on the fact that my very own big sister, the one who was more patient with me than anyone else in the whole wide world, was missing. With a book you could always peek at the final page if the suspense proved to be too much. In real life, the final page had not yet been written.

And so, even though I felt a little guilty, I was really excited to hear that Daddy had planned an adventure for us that promised only carefree fun.

18

When June twentieth came, everyone showed up at our house, and we all piled into our Chevy station wagon. The trailer was hitched to the car, the brake lights connected and tested, and off we went. There were a total of twelve people in the car that day. We were all smushed together, but at that time in America, cramming ten kids into a station wagon was not considered a crime.

When we arrived at our campsite, right on the shore of the Puget Sound, we all spilled out of the car and ran to the water's edge. There was green seaweed lying stranded all over the beach. I picked some of it up. It was slimy and rubbery and it had bubbles that were full of some kind of fluid. I squeezed the bubbles, but I couldn't pop them. I noticed then that the seaweed had a weird smell. I quickly dropped it and then held my hands up to my nose – my hands smelled like fish. I looked over at Scottie just then and he was dropping the blob of seaweed that he had just picked up. "Peeee-uuuuuu!" he exclaimed, and I laughed.

The weather was absolutely perfect. It was a beautiful day, and the theme song to a popular TV show started to run through my head. I couldn't help myself – I burst out singing:

The bluest skies you've ever seen – in Seattle!

Adele's friends started laughing, but then they all joined me:

And the hills, the greenest green – in Seattle!
Like a beautiful child growing up free and wild;
Full of hopes and full of fears,
Full of laughter full of tears,
Full of dreams to last the years –
In Seattle, in Seattle!

We were all turning round and round on the beach as we belted out the song. When we had finished singing, some of the girls fell down laughing, and then we all ended up on our backs in the sand, staring up into the deep blue sky as the world twirled around us dizzily.

"I love Bobby Sherman," one of the girls, Marty, said. He was one of the stars on the show *Here Come the Brides.* The song that we had just sung was the theme song for that show. The other girls all laughed and agreed that he was dreamy.

"Who do you like more," one of the girls asked, "Bobby Sherman, Davy Jones, or David Cassidy?" Wow, that was a hard one. I was personally in love with all three of them, and also Greg Brady, but I didn't dare open my mouth and admit this. Marty started to sing again:

> *I think I love you – so what am I so afraid of?*

We all joined in the chorus of the song that David Cassidy sang:

> *I'm afraid that I'm not sure of –*
> *A love there is no cure for.*
> *I think I love you – isn't that what life is made of?*
> *Though it worries me to say, that I never felt this way!*

My dad had actually taken Angela, Adele and me to a David Cassidy concert that year. I was shocked when he said he had tickets because, up until that time, I had rarely even heard a secular song played in our house, and then, only when my parents weren't home.

We had grown up on the Blackwood Brothers Quartet and, as we got older, we were allowed to listen to the Imperials, a Christian 'rock' group – but never, *ever* could we change the radio dial to a popular station. Once I overheard Graham complain to Angela about not being allowed to listen to good music in our house, but I didn't understand what he was talking about – I liked the Imperials.

When our music teacher at school taught us two popular songs from the radio – *Horse with No Name* and *I Can See Clearly Now, the Rain is Gone* – for some reason, I felt guilty singing them. I would mouth the words to the songs as we sang them in class because I didn't want to get in trouble, but I felt that I would be disobeying my parents – or maybe even God – if I actually sang the words out loud.

So, when my dad told us that he was taking us to a David Cassidy concert, for a minute I was afraid that he was backsliding. But in spite of my worries, I went to the concert and I loved it. As we were driving home in the car, all three of us girls argued over who David had been pointing to when he sang the words 'I think I love you'. Personally, I knew that he had pointed to me.

၁ ၁

"Hey, Girls," my dad called out to us. "Come and get your buckets and spades. We're going to dig for geoducks!" We all got up and ran over to my parents.

"What's a *gooey-duck*?" my sister's friend, Jo Jo, asked.

"Yeah," Scottie said, and then started quacking. My dad laughed.

"You don't know what a geoduck is?" he asked, acting surprised. I laughed.

"Yeah, Jo Jo," I said, "you don't know what a gooey-duck is?" Of course, I was secretly thinking, what is a gooey-duck?

"Bobbi," Graham said, jumping to Jo Jo's defense, "if you know what a geoduck is, then spell it." It sounded like a trick question, so I kept my mouth shut.

"I know," Scottie shouted, "G-O-O-O-O..." We all started laughing. Graham then spelled it for us the right way, and I was glad I hadn't attempted it.

"Geoducks aren't really ducks at all," my dad explained. "They're actually huge clams. They are so big, in fact, we only have to find one to make chowder for all of us!"

"Cool!" "Really?" "Gross!" All the girls had different responses to the idea of finding a gigantic clam crawling around in the sand. I was thinking that I wanted to find the first one.

"How do we catch them, Daddy?" Adele asked. I was pretty sure that she wanted to find the first one, too. She had that look in her eye...

"Okay. Here's what we're going to be doing. We'll actually be looking for regular clams *and* geoducks." We all nodded our heads as he continued. "Clams spit water up into the air. When they do this, little bubbles appear in the sand. Let's spread out over the beach here, and look closely for those little bubbles."

"Here are some bubbles," Scottie yelled.

"Okay, Son, grab your shovel and start digging," my dad yelled back. He had given every one of us a shovel and a pail. Scottie dropped to his knees and took his spade and started to dig. He uncovered a squirming little shell and grabbed it with his hand.

"I caught one!" Scottie shouted as he jumped up and held out his find for all of us to see. "It's a baby geoduck," he said. He was so happy he did a little dance.

"Good for you, Scottie," my dad said encouragingly. "That's probably just a regular clam. Geoducks are usually buried really, really deep, and they are about eight inches long," he explained, holding his hands apart to show us. The clam that Scottie was holding was only about one inch long.

"When a geoduck spits, the water will go a couple of feet up in the air, so you'll know it's no regular clam. But any clam is fair game today. Put that one in your bucket, Scottie. And, girls, on your mark, get set, go. First one to fill their bucket gets a prize!"

And we were off. Once we started to really look, we noticed that there were air bubbles all over the seashore. What a day. We caught clam after clam after clam. Happily, it was Adele, the birthday girl, who filled her bucket first. She was so excited. Her face was red again, but this time it was because of exertion and joy, not pain. I was glad for her.

"Way to go, Princess," my dad exclaimed when Adele had presented her full bucket to him. "Go give them to your mom." Mom was sitting in front of the Coleman stove, pumping air into the small gas tank to keep the flame burning. She already had a pot of coffee percolating and a kettle of water coming to a boil.

"Adele, this is wonderful," my mom said to her birthday girl. "We are going to make the best clam chowder ever."

"Thank you, Mommy," my sister said, and the two of them looked at each other long and hard. I had to look away or I knew that I was going to start crying.

None of us actually caught a geoduck that day. We didn't even see real evidence that they existed. But, as my mom was cooking up what we did catch, my dad told us the amazing story of the geoduck.

"Geoducks are called the elephant trunk clam in Asia," he said. "They are considered a great delicacy, especially in Japan, but they can only be found and harvested right here in the Pacific Northwest."

"Daddy, are you making this up?" I asked. My father was a great story-teller, and I wanted to be sure that this was a true story, because as soon as school started I was going to tell everyone who would listen about the giant clams that lived right under Seattle's shoreline.

"No, Honey. This is true, cross my heart. I learned about them in my science class this year. Now, to be sure, the geoduck is probably one of the most revolting edible creatures on the face of the earth. I read somewhere that people think that it must have been created on one of God's off days because it is so ugly!" My dad laughed at the thought.

"But, apparently, the taste of geoduck chowder is amazing," he continued. "It may be scary looking, but it is delicious." Dad was making us all hungry. As I watched my mom stir the soup on our green portable stove, I found myself hoping that regular clam chowder was going to be as good as geoduck chowder.

"The geoduck usually stays deep in the sandy beds beneath the ocean. It is only at low tides that its presence can be detected," my dad explained. "And even then, it is not easy to catch." As I was listening to my dad, I made a silent vow to myself that someday I would come back and actually catch a geoduck.

While we were clam digging, my dad and Graham had built a roaring fire. All of us girls were now huddled close to it, blankets wrapped around our shoulders, drowsily listening to Daddy's words. It was kind of surreal to be thinking about magical creatures that really existed right under us. I imagined that one might be underneath us at that very moment, several feet below the sand. It was nice, kind of like a fairy tale, and I wished that we could stay at the beach forever.

My mom's clam chowder was the best thing that I had ever tasted in my entire life. I ate so much that I felt like I was going to pop. She put out oyster crackers and cheese and all kinds of fruit. We had a feast on the beach that evening, and we were giddy and content as the sun dropped out of sight.

19

Seattle has never been known for its warm weather, even in June, and as the sun disappeared, we were grateful for the big bonfire. Graham began to tell ghost stories. All of Adele's girlfriends pretended to be scared out of their minds and they moved closer to him for safety. I actually *was* getting frightened as he told one haunting tale after another. I had never liked ghost stories before, but now, with Angela missing, they were more than scary – they were threatening. The thing was, I knew that the devil existed, and it was hard not to think that he was behind all the trouble we were going through. I guess that Daddy thought that Graham's tales were harmless, so he didn't stop him from telling them. But after the second story, I casually got up from where I was and went to sit right next to my dad. He very obligingly wrapped his arms around me and, for a brief time, I felt safe.

My parents finally made us go to bed. Adele and her girlfriends all got to sleep in the pop-up trailer. I was really hoping that I could sleep there with them. But Lizzie, Scottie, Graham, my mom and dad – and I – had to sleep in the regular tent. But that was okay. It was Adele's birthday, after all. I had been asleep for awhile when I turned onto my back and was aware of a sloshing noise. 'What in the world?' I thought as I straightened my legs out. My sleeping bag was soaking wet. The first thing I thought was that I had wet my pants – how embarrassing! But as I became more awake, I realized that even my feet were wet. I was sleeping in a puddle of water. It was then that I heard the steady pitter-patter of rain on the canvas over my head.

"Daddy," I mumbled, "it's raining."

"Huh? What?" I could hear my dad slowly coming to his senses. I didn't want to wake him up, but I had to – I was freezing!

"I'm soaking wet, Daddy!" I said. By this time my mom had awakened too.

"What's the matter?" she asked. I guess that the water hadn't reached the area where they were sleeping. As soon as I heard my mom's voice, my resolve fell away.

"Mommy, I'm wet!" I cried.

"Shhh!" she hushed. "Let's not wake everybody up. Are you really wet? Get out of your sleeping bag and come over here." I tried to pull my sodden legs out of the heavy sleeping bag, but it was as thoroughly wet as was I. When I had finally extracted my body from the clinging material, I crawled over to my mom. She reached out and touched my leg.

"Ew, yuck," she said, "You *are* wet, Honey."

"And I'm freezing," I whined. I couldn't help myself. What was it about mothers that made a grown girl turn into a baby?

"Okay, it's okay," she said soothingly. "Let's get you out of those wet clothes."

"No!" I replied. After all, Graham, Scottie and Daddy were in the tent. I would not take one piece of clothing off of my body unless I was sure that their eyes weren't open.

"Oh, for goodness sake, Bobbi, no one is looking at you! It's pitch dark, for one thing." I was making my mom mad, which was not a good idea. It was time to peel off my wet pajamas.

"I don't know where my other clothes are," I said.

"Just get in my sleeping bag," she said. "Hurry up or you'll catch your death of cold." I wriggled my naked little body into my mom's big sleeping bag, feeling absolutely mortified. My mom slipped out of the sleeping bag and foraged around in the dark, looking for some dry clothes for me. She finally came back with a shirt and some pants, but no underwear whatsoever. It felt kind of weird putting on clothes with no underwear, but I was not about to argue with my mom. She got back into bed with me and that's the last thing I remember.

In the morning, we all woke up to find that my sleeping bag was completely under water! The rest of us were on high enough ground that the water never reached us, and the girls, of course, were safe in their trailer, so no real harm had been done by the rain. Once everyone was awake, my dad sent all the kids into the woods around the shore to find some firewood. I waited until the tent was empty, and then I found a pair of dry panties and an undershirt. I crawled back into my parent's sleeping bag and got undressed and then put all of my clothes back on. I was not about to go out in public without any underwear on.

It was cold that June morning, and my mom had packed my long, clingy, polyester pants, and a sweatshirt with a hood, so that I could tie it tightly around my face. When I joined the others, they were hurrying to get their task done because the thought of a roaring campfire beckoned them. By the time we had gathered the wood, my mom had already put on a pot of coffee, and she was making us eggs, sausage and bacon on her little gas stove. The fire we made on the beach that morning was huge, and it brought a rosy glow to all of our faces. We ate our breakfast and then we all spread out and practiced our cartwheels and round-offs on the pebbly shore.

Adele's birthday party was a huge success. The girls had a wonderful time, and everyone in our family was given, for a brief moment, the lovely sense that everything was right in the world. It was hard to face what we saw once we got back to the house.

The policemen who were overseeing Angela's case had made themselves at home. We returned to dirty coffee cups all over the living room and kitchen, overflowing waste baskets, and the toilet seat left in the upright position. I was personally kind of happy to see that there were men still working on the case even while Scottie and Lizzie and I had taken a break. The rest of the family, on the other hand, felt intruded upon. My brothers and sister quickly disappeared to their rooms and shut the doors. It wasn't that they were ungrateful – my parents were deeply appreciative that the Seattle Police Department was determined to find our Angela, and they told Uncle Roy that over and over. But I could see it in their faces. There was a haunted look in their eyes that they tried to cover over with smiles that looked forced.

I wanted to be involved in the conversations that took place between the police and my parents, but I was not invited to join them in their debriefing session. As a result, I was forced to eavesdrop. The policemen invited my parents to sit down in the living room while they caught them up on everything that had happened during the day and a half that we had been gone. I was sitting on the kitchen floor, pressing my ear against the swinging door that separated the kitchen from the living room. Unfortunately, no one in the living room had learned the importance of speaking clearly.

By the time I was ten, I had already been in four Christmas plays. The director had told us to enunciate in every one of them.

"No one will be able to hear you if you do not speak slowly and loudly," he emphasized. "You may as well not say anything at all if what you say cannot be heard by every parent in the audience. *Enunciate!*" We all rolled our eyes when we heard that speech, but now, as I pressed my ear to the solid wooden door, desperately trying to make out what they were saying, I found myself thinking, 'Come on, You Guys – enunciate!'

All I was able to hear was that tests were being done, that the tire tracks were being looked into, and that the sizes of the shoes were women's six and men's eleven. Well, that was something. Angela wore a size six shoe. But that was basically it. There had been no phone calls. No body had been found... I was very happy to hear that. As I sat down on the old, cracked, blue and white linoleum kitchen floor, I thanked God that no body had been found.

20

The first thing that I remember about the next day, Sunday morning, was the smell of coffee luring me from my dreams. I had always loved the smell of coffee – probably because my mom kept a pot percolating at all times of the day. I can remember my grandpa, Robert, who I got my name from, drinking a full cup of black coffee at the end of a long day. He said it helped him sleep at night. And so, it was the aroma of Maxwell House that woke me up that day. I didn't open my eyes for a while. I just stayed on my back with my covers pulled up over my face and enjoyed the feeling of being half awake and half asleep. I slept all the way under the covers when we lived in Seattle because our tiny room was drafty. No matter if it was summer or winter, I always felt just a little bit chilly.

I was still cozy with sleep that morning and I had a smile on my face as I thought about the fun we'd had on our camping trip. It was on a camping trip that I had initially learned to like coffee. At first, I just held the cup for warmth, but eventually, I tasted it. As I lay in my bed, I suddenly remembered that it was Sunday, and that we would be going to church again without Angela.

Sundays were hard – face after face would pass by me saying, 'Have you heard anything?' or 'So sad, so sad' or 'Well, you know that we are praying for her'... Everyone was nice. So nice, in fact, that it made me break down and cry, and I hated to cry, period, let alone in front of a bunch of people. I think the hardest thing about going to church without Angela was seeing her boyfriend, Tom Walters. He had been dating her for about six months. He was a really sweet boy; I heard my mom say so. And he was cute; nobody had to tell me that. Tom was about six feet tall, which made him tower over little five-foot-three Angela. It was like they were exact opposites: Tom was tall, Angela was tiny; Tom had blonde hair, Angela's hair was dark brown; Tom's eyes were blue, while Angela's were the color of chocolate. The only trait they shared was that they both had a natural curl in their hair. I liked to think about how cute their children were going to be – for sure, they would have curly hair. I knew that they were going to get married because they held hands all the time, and once I saw them kissing outside by the tree when Tom was dropping Angela off after one of their dates.

My parents liked Tom. Before asking Angela out, he went to my dad first to ask him for his permission. And each time they went on a date, Tom would first come into the house and chat with my parents. After they left, my mom would always comment, "He's such a nice boy."

I would try to be there when Tom rang the doorbell. "Hi, Tom," I'd greet him as he'd come into the living room. "Angela's not quite ready yet, ya wanna sit down? Or, we could go out and play catch, if you want?" Tom was the pitcher of his high school varsity baseball team, and he was only a sophomore! He really liked to play catch with me, or at least, he rarely told me no when I asked him. Sometimes my parents would shoo me away, and sometimes Angela would get ready too fast and we didn't have time to play, but he would always assure me that there would be a next time.

One Saturday, Tom came over to our house early just to hang out and be with Angela. But my dad already had other plans. He announced that he wanted to take us downtown to visit Pike Place Market. Tom said it sounded like fun and agreed to come along with the rest of the family.

My dad was always coming up with ways to spend our Saturdays, which I loved because then we didn't have to clean the house and do other chores. As a college student, he was exposed to a lot of very hip things that probably the average thirty-four-year-old dad wouldn't have been aware of. He would hear the other students talking about the market downtown, or a concert and fireworks show near Green Lake, and he'd come home and tell us about it. In fact, the week after we moved from Richland, he took us down to the Seattle Center for a music festival. It was crazy. We parked our car next to a split-window VW van. There were big orange and purple flowers and peace signs painted all over it. We kids peeked inside and saw that it had a little sink and a bed. It was so cool.

I heard that there were more than a hundred thousand people gathered for the festival. My dad hadn't realized that it was going to be such a huge event. He had just seen a cardboard poster on a telephone pole. It was yellow and purplish and it showed a closed fist with a thumb pointing to the sky and the words said "Fun for Everyone." That's all the promotion my dad had needed. They called the event *Festival '71* and it was really fun in a scary kind of way. The music was booming through big speakers. Most of the people who had come to the festival were pretty weird looking. It seemed like every man had hair as long as Adele's and, let's just say, I was not the only girl there who apparently was not allowed to wear a bra. But Daddy was right there with us so we were safe. It was very exciting.

On the Saturday morning that our dad took us to the market, Tom had decided to squeeze into the station wagon with us. Scottie and I were stuck in the back, as always, sitting on the floor and hunching over so our heads wouldn't bump the roof. Daddy pulled out of our driveway, and soon we were on Aurora Avenue heading toward Pike Place. The size of Seattle never failed to amaze me. Richland's downtown only had four stores, so downtown Seattle seemed huge to me. I'll never forget the first time I saw the monorail, and the Seattle Space Needle.

We parked near the market, on Western Avenue. The thing that impressed me the most was the number of people there, and it wasn't even a holiday or anything. I loved crowds. It was fun being jostled by the streams of peculiar looking people, fun hearing all the different languages that were being spoken, and fun breathing in the exotic, fair-like aromas. There was a mixture of garlic and onions and sausages in the air, and sweet things like cinnamon rolls and cotton candy and taffy. I closed my eyes and took in a big whiff of it. The smells made me heady. Lizzie hadn't arrived in Seattle yet, so my partner that day was Scottie. He grabbed my elbow and told me to hurry up and follow him. As my parents yelled out to us to stick close to them, we ran into the marketplace, staying way ahead of the rest of our family for most of the day.

The first thing that Scottie and I saw once we got into the market was an assortment of great big fishes laid out on ice. All the signs read 'Fresh Fish'. And fresh they were, poor things. The fish looked like they were still breathing and their eyeballs seemed to be focusing on the people who were milling about. They were truly straight off the boat. But even as fresh as they were, they still smelled like fish.

"Yuck," Scottie said as he plugged his nose. I made a grimace and plugged my nose too. We were standing there pretending to gag when Tom and Angela caught up to us.

"Hey, Angela," Scottie called out, "take a whiff – peeee-uuuuuu!" I started laughing, my nose still firmly gripped between my thumb and forefinger.

"You Guys!" Angela ran up to me and pulled my hand away from my face. She looked around to see if Tom had noticed us. Who would have thought that our behavior would embarrass Angela? It was one of those moments when I was just a bit too young to realize what I had done wrong, but I was old enough to know that it must have been really stupid. Scottie was still plugging his nose and acting like the smell was going to kill him, but I just stood there.

Finally, I said, "Scottie, cut it out!" He just looked at me like, 'What's wrong with you?' I felt a little like a traitor, but Tom was standing right there, and I didn't want him to think that I was immature. I rolled my eyes at Scottie and then looked at Tom as if to say 'kids'. But Tom just pinched his nose and put Scottie in a headlock.

"It does stink around here, doesn't it, Scottie?" Tom said. Scottie loved that. He grabbed Tom's arm and they started to fake wrestle. I felt jealous and a little torn; somehow being mature didn't seem to impress Tom, and I was left out of the fun. But I think Angela was relieved that I was standing still and quiet next to her, so that at least was a good thing. I didn't really blame Angela for being mad at Scottie and me. After all, she was going out with the love of her life, and we could have easily messed things up for her. I knew that Angela and Tom were truly in love, because, besides the fact that I had caught them kissing, I had also accidentally found some notes that Angela had received from Tom, and I had, well, I had more or less read some of them – okay, most of them. In my defense, Angela left her notes in a shoebox on the floor next to her bed. It wasn't like she was trying to hide them or anything.

The first notes were kind of formal: "I really enjoyed spending time with you today, Angela, you make me laugh." And, "My friends think you're really funny, Angela. I told them to stay away from you. Ha! But seriously, I had fun, and you looked really pretty. I like the way you wear your hair." But after a while, the notes got more personal: "I feel like I'm the luckiest guy in the world. You are so beautiful and smart! Thank you for helping me with my geometry." And then, "No one has ever made me laugh the way you make me laugh. I miss you tonight. Did I ever tell you how good you smell?" And, "I know that I just said good-bye to you on the phone, but I can't help myself. I have to tell you that

I'm still thinking of you. I think I'm going to go sit in my car for a while because it smells like your perfume."

I felt a little guilty for reading their private notes, but I couldn't help myself. They just got better and better. They were a lot more interesting than a *Hardy Boys* book. "You are the first girl that I have ever felt this way about, Angela, and I want you to know that I think that I love you. No, I know that I love you, with all of my heart."

Tom told Angela that he dreamed about either becoming a professional baseball player or getting into medical school – once he had accomplished one of these goals, he would ask Angela to marry him. I felt like I was going to explode with happiness when I read that note. How could Angela be keeping this stuff a secret? Didn't she know that we would be going crazy with excitement for her?

I had been reading one note after the other for over an hour, and there were only a few more, but I was afraid that Angela would catch me in her room, so I put the notes back exactly where I had found them, and I slipped out of the room. I had never in my life read anything more romantic or more exciting than the notes that Tom had written to my sister, Angela. I climbed up into my tree house and closed my eyes and dreamed about the day when somebody, maybe Jimmy, would write love letters to me. Or maybe he would keep a journal of all his deepest, most romantic thoughts, and I would discover the journal and find out how he really felt about me – kind of like that song that Angela always played on the record player:

> *I found her diary underneath a tree,*
>
> *And started reading about me.*
>
> *The words she'd written took me by surprise;*
>
> *You'd never read them in her eyes.*
>
> *They said that she had found the love she'd waited for;*
>
> *Wouldn't you know it, she wouldn't show it.*

I couldn't remember the rest of the words, but I loved that song. It was so romantic, but I think it might have had a sad ending. I'd have to ask Angela; she had every song on that Bread album memorized.

By that time my entire family had caught up to us, so we went back to exploring the marketplace. The good thing about Scottie was that he didn't hold a grudge. He could've decided that he didn't want to play with me for the rest of the day. After all, I had kind of betrayed him back there, but he chose to pretend like he hadn't noticed, and so we were off again, like Lewis and Clark, forging a path for the rest of our family to follow.

Scottie and I were enthralled with the marketplace. There were fish, of course, but there were also Indian wares like totem poles, and miniature tepees, and rugs, and animal skins. My father's grandfather was a full-blooded Cherokee, so we were always interested in Indian stuff. I had been really wanting a pair of moccasins for my birthday. I looked back to see if I could see my mom. I hoped that maybe she would find a pair for me... There were other kinds of shops, too – shops that had cheeses and jellies and all kinds of pickled things. We explored until we were exhausted and hungry, and then we went back and found the rest of the family. Our parents told us to head back to the car. We couldn't afford to buy lunch for all of us at the market, but my mom had packed apples for us to eat on the way home. As we were making our way back to our parking space, we came upon a store that smelled of fresh coffee.

"Oh, Daddy – let's go into this store," my mom said. "It smells so good." And it did smell good. We all filed into the store and Scottie and I were quick to notice that they were giving out small cups of coffee to sample. We quickly lined up to get our free cup.

"Is it okay with your parents for you kids to sample coffee?" asked the guy standing behind the counter. He was wearing a white apron with the word 'Zev' stitched on it. We weren't sure if he was mad at us or if that's the way he always sounded.

"I think it's okay. They let us have it at home," I said, looking back at my parents. My mother was on the other side of the shop, looking at some fancy coffee machines that were lined up on the shelves. My dad was intrigued by a bunch of boat stuff that was on another wall.

"Hey, folks. Is it okay with you if I give your kids a sample of one of our richest, dark-roasted coffees?" Zev called out to our parents. Both my mom and dad looked a bit embarrassed for a moment, but as they walked over to talk to the coffee guy, the smile on his face seemed to put them at ease.

"Is it okay with you?" my mother asked him tentatively.

"Sure, it's fine with me. Gotta start 'em off on the good stuff, right?" Zev laughed to himself. "Here. Why don't the two of you try some of this brew? We just roasted these beans about an hour ago."

My parents were only too thrilled to sample the rich-smelling coffee, and they accepted the small cups and blew on them for a minute before they each took a sip. They drank their coffee black; we, on the other hand put three cubes of sugar each into our little paper cups, along with a hefty portion of cream. As we walked away from the counter, I saw Scottie grab two more cubes and put them in his pocket to suck on later. I wished that he had grabbed some for me.

"Wow," my dad said, "this is good coffee!" My mom nodded her head in agreement. Scottie and I took a sip. It was different – strong, but with a slightly bitter aftertaste. I liked it, but not as much as I liked my mom's coffee.

"Bobbi, come here," Scottie whispered. "Look at this," he giggled. Scottie was looking at a painting of a mermaid on the window in the front of the shop. The mermaid was buck naked and her mermaid tail was split in two. She was holding both ends of the tail with out-stretched arms. Scottie was staring right at her bare breasts. I grabbed his arm and pulled him away from the window and told him to close his eyes.

"That's disgusting," I said, but he just grinned at me. I frowned back. "Scott Johnson," I said, "sometimes I worry about you." I walked over to my parents. Zev was talking to them.

"How would you like to buy a pound of some of these freshly roasted coffee beans? And could I interest you in a coffee grinder, or do you two already have one at home?" Zev asked. I guess he wanted us to buy something; after all, we had just drunk eight cups of his coffee, for free. My mother looked interested, but then she noticed the price.

"A dollar and seventy-five cents for a pound of coffee?" she whispered to Daddy. "I can get five pounds of Maxwell House for that on sale at Safeway!" My father put his arm around her shoulder and then smiled at the man behind the counter.

"I think we'll pass today," my dad said politely. "This was sure good coffee, though. Thank you for the samples, Zev." Daddy always used a person's name when he talked to them. I liked that about him. The man just nodded his head and looked over my dad's shoulder at the next person in line. We followed my parents out of the store, and I stole another look at the logo on the window. The name of the store was spelled out around the naked mermaid. It said 'Starbucks'.

"That store will not be able to stay in business," my mom declared emphatically. "Can you imagine charging a dollar-seventy-five for a pound of coffee?" My dad just hugged her and kissed her on the cheek.

"I like your coffee best, anyway, Sweetheart."

かど めん

On that Sunday morning, I saw Tom standing with a bunch of teenagers. Two of the teenagers were girls and it looked to me like they were trying just a little bit too hard to make him feel better. Tom caught me looking at him, and he called out for me to come over to where they were standing.

"Hi," I said, feeling very aware of how young I must have looked to Tom compared to those two sixteen-year-old girls. Plus, the night before, after my bath, my mom had decided to cut off all of my hair. She told me it was a "Pixie cut" and that I would look adorable, but I just think that she was tired of having to help me untangle my long, coarse, curly hair every time I washed it – so off it came. I looked like a little boy that morning, and I knew it.

"Hey, Kid. I like your new look," Tom said as he reached over and tousled my newly-shorn curls. I felt the blood rushing up my cheeks and – for some reason – tears popped into my eyes. I turned around quickly to hide my face, but Tom grabbed my arm and pulled me into a hug.

"Hey, it's okay. It seems all I ever do is cry these days, too." I was furiously mopping the tears off of my face even as he was hugging me. The bad thing was that I wasn't exactly sure that he and I were crying for the same reason, and it made me feel guilty for a second.

I mean, of course I was crying over Angela. I had never stopped crying over Angela, but this time, I think that I was really crying because it felt so good to have this handsome big boy notice me and be nice to me. Surely there was something wrong with that, something wrong with me, wasn't there?

I mumbled something under my breath and then made a beeline for the girl's bathroom where I immediately locked myself into one of the stalls. Lizzie must have been watching the whole thing because, in a minute, I heard the bathroom door open.

"Are you okay, Bobbi?" she asked. I'm pretty sure that I had never loved anyone more in my life than I loved Lizzie Ann Gardiner at that moment. Here she was, on her vacation, and she was spending all of her time worrying and crying and comforting me and my family. Another girl would have asked to go home the minute the fun had stopped. But she was my friend, my true-blue friend.

21

When we got home from church that Sunday, we heard the phone ringing as we were getting out of the car. There were policemen upstairs, monitoring all of our calls, so we didn't hurry to answer it. Once we got inside, they held their fingers up to their mouths as if to shush us. We all moved into the living room and silently sat down. Uncle Roy was on the phone.

"Yes, yes, that's right. Yes, okay. Where was that again?" He motioned with his hands for someone to get him a pen and a pad. "Okay, I'm ready. Uh-huh, I got it. What is it you want? How much?" he asked. "Tomorrow at ten in the morning. Just me. Hello? Hello?" Uncle Roy pushed on the receiver again and again and then put the phone in its cradle. "Well, folks, I don't know if this is for real, but it appears that our abductor has finally made contact." Cheers went up among the men in blue who had been hanging on to every word that Uncle Roy was saying into the phone.

"What are their demands?" one of the policemen asked.

"Well, that's the thing," Uncle Roy said. He stopped talking abruptly, as if he had suddenly become aware of our presence. Uncle Roy cleared his throat, and then gave my parents a look. I knew that he was trying to say, 'Can you please get rid of these kids?' I decided to help him out.

"Hey," I suggested, "why don't we go play dominoes while Mom makes dinner? Huh?"

"I don't feel like playing dominoes," Scottie whined.

"Sure you do," Graham chimed in, "you love dominoes, Scottie. Or would you rather set the table?" Graham had grabbed Scottie's arms and was trying to lift him up over his head.

"Nah. I don't want to set the table. I want to wrestle. Come on, Graham." As my parents walked into the kitchen with Uncle Roy, Scottie tackled Graham, and they ended up on the living room floor, rolling around. It looked like fun – for a moment, I wanted to be a boy too, so I could wrestle with my brothers on the floor.

"Come on, Bobbi and Lizzie," Adele said, "I'll play dominoes with you." I smiled at her. I didn't really want to play dominoes. I had just made that up to get the kids out of the kitchen, but Adele was doing her best to make everyone around her happy. If she thought that I wanted to play, then she would.

"It's okay, Adele," I said, "but would you mind if Lizzie and I just hung out with you for awhile?" Adele didn't seem to know what to say to that request. "You could, like, paint our nails or something, couldn't you?" Adele and Lizzie both stared at me. Adele cocked her head to one side.

"You would let me paint your nails?" she asked. In the past, when Adele suggested that it might be fun to do nails and hair, I had wanted nothing to do with it, but things had changed lately. On the one hand, I would've given anything to have thrown myself on the floor to wrestle with the boys. On the other hand, and maybe it was because of my boy haircut, but, looking pretty suddenly appealed to me.

"Yeah, I'll let you paint my nails," I said to Adele.

"Oh, Bobbi, we'll have so much fun – come over here!" Adele shrieked. "Angela and I just got two new colors, Peony Pink and Tangy Tangerine! I think you'd look beautiful in the pink." It was obvious that Adele had really been missing Angela. "By the way, you look adorable with your new Pixie hairdo," Adele said. I reached up and ran both of my hands through my remaining locks, feeling shocked once again at how light my head felt. I was pretty sure that my mom had made Adele say those exact words to me, but I was hoping that she really meant what she said.

"Thanks, Adele."

"What color do you want, Lizzie?" Adele asked. "We can use the pink on you too, if you want. Or, just a minute..." Adele disappeared into the closet that she and Angela shared and came out a second later carrying a bucket full of nail polish bottles.

"You can have your pick!" The look on Adele's face at that moment was one of pure joy. She had been holding up really well over the last two weeks, but she was in need of some beauty therapy, and I was glad that Lizzie and I were there to meet her needs.

Even as Adele was painting Peony Pink on my nails, I could not help but wonder what was going on in the kitchen. What did Uncle Roy mean when he said that he hoped it was the real thing? Why else would someone contact us, unless they knew something?

I couldn't possibly imagine. I was hoping that I would be able to get Uncle Roy alone for a minute that night, and that I could convince him to fill me in on the latest. But as hard as I tried, I could not seem to convey the message to Uncle Roy – or any of the Seattle Police Department – that I really needed to speak with one of them.

After our beauty session was over, I made my way into the living room, where all the men were talking under their breath. I stood there, waiting to be invited into the circle, but no one would even look at me.

"Where is Uncle Roy?" I finally resorted to asking one of the guys.

"Why do you want to know?" he asked me. I felt really frustrated. Didn't these guys know that we kids had led them to their first clue? I put my hands on my hips.

"Because," I replied, "I think he just might need me to help him tomorrow." All the policemen broke out laughing, which made me even madder.

"Just tell me where he is!" I blurted out, trying my best not to cry.

"Okay, Kid, calm down. I think Roy is outside, talking to your dad." I turned and walked out of the room with purpose, but I could hear the men chuckling as I left. I knew that my cheeks were pink when I got outside, so I waited for a second before walking over to my parents and Uncle Roy. I nudged my way into their circle, and looked up expectantly at the three of them.

"Honey," my mother said distractedly, "have you practiced your piano yet?" I looked at her with my sweetest, most compliant look.

"I was just about to," I replied, crossing my fingers.

"Why don't you go and do that right now," she said, shooing me away with a gentle push. "That's a good girl." There was no arguing with my mother, so I turned around and walked back into the house. All of us kids were required to practice the piano for thirty minutes every day. As I pulled my music out and placed it on the piano, I found myself envying Angela for just a minute. She hadn't had to practice for weeks! But as soon as the thought entered my mind, I felt terrible.

"Oh, Lord, forgive me. I'll practice a whole hour a day if you'll just bring Angela back to us!"

We had been taking piano lessons for as long as I could remember. When we lived in Richland, our teacher had been Mrs. Corder. Now that we lived in Seattle, we took lessons from Mrs. Laurent. I'm not really sure how my mom found her, but she was supposed to be one of the best piano teachers in the Seattle area. She lived on Mercer Island, which was a long, long ride from our home. My mom would drive us for what seemed like an hour through the city. We knew we were almost there when we got to the floating bridge. The bridge was always the best part of the drive. Our dad told us that the Mercer Island Floating Bridge opened in 1940, and that it was the very first floating bridge ever built. Just the thought of driving over something that was the first of its kind gave me a thrill.

Back in the olden days, people went over to the island to pick berries. I figured it must have been blackberries, because there were bunches of blackberry bushes in Mrs. Laurent's yard. It was the Indians who would row the white people over Lake Washington to the island, and then row them back at the end of the day. Indians didn't live on the island because they thought there were evil spirits there. One of the first berry pickers was a man named Thomas Mercer, and that's who the island ended up being named after. When I found that out, I remember thinking how unfair it was. After all, the Indians were there first, and the island should have been named after one of them. I probably felt that way because of my Cherokee roots.

Once we got to Mrs. Laurent's house, we would each take our lesson, one after the other. Four of us had a half-hour lesson, and one had a forty-five minute lesson. When one of us was with Mrs. Laurent, the rest of us were left to our own devices. Her house was more like a museum than a home. I never knew if Mrs. Laurent was married or had children, but I was pretty sure not. My mom would remind us every week not to touch anything in the house.

"Just go outside and down to the lake, and be careful," she always told us. Never mind that it was raining or had just rained – after all, it was Seattle – but we were kids, and there were a million things to do to have fun. Mrs. Laurent had a trail leading down through the woods right to the waterfront, and she had a boat ramp with a canoe tied to it. Lake Washington was beautiful and Mercer Island was a really nice place to live. I remember my mom telling my dad that Mrs. Laurent's house had cost her forty-nine thousand dollars. Our house in Richland had cost my parents seventeen thousand dollars, so I knew that Mrs. Laurent must have been rich. Even though I hated to practice, I always thought that I should become a piano teacher so that I could be rich and live on a lake, too, when I grew up.

Mrs. Laurent had only taken all of us on because of the potential that she had seen in my brother, Graham. Graham was the one who had the forty-five minute lesson. She suffered through four thirty-minute lessons with the rest of us because those were the conditions that my mother had set up. I had taken lessons in Richland for two years and had advanced to the John Thompson book, Level 4, which I thought was pretty good. My parents had been pleased with my progress – that is, until I started taking lessons with Mrs. Laurent. After three sessions, she asked my mother to join us.

"This child does not read music," Mrs. Laurent declared. My mother looked at me with shock and horror. 'Not read music? No!' she seemed to be screaming at me.

"It's true, Mrs. Johnson," Mrs. Laurent said accusingly, "she requests that I play every piece for her, and then she repeats what I have played. I'm afraid to tell you, but Roberta is playing by ear!"

How humiliating. I had been found out. It was true – I had never bothered to learn to read music. I had discovered in the beginning of my music career that I could pretty much copy what I heard being played. So, I just made sure that my teacher played the song once through. I had gotten away with it so far, but Mrs. Laurent was too smart for me.

"If Roberta does not come back next week reading music, then I am afraid that I will have to drop her." What? Was she allowed to drop me? I thought that we were paying her to teach me – how could she drop me? I was outraged, but my mother seemed to think that Mrs. Laurent was being very reasonable, and she agreed to her demands. On the way home that day, my mother spoke very sternly to me.

"Bobbi, I am going to pay Adele twenty-five cents an hour to teach you how to read music. If you don't learn in one week, then not only will you be dropped by Mrs. Laurent, but you will have to pay Adele back for her time, out of your savings account." My mom knew how precious my savings account was to me. I had carefully deposited most of my allowance in there for years, and the balance of my passbook was nearly thirty-five dollars.

I was feeling desperate on many levels. I didn't think that it was possible for me to learn how to read music that quickly, but I did not want to be the only Johnson child who couldn't play the piano. And I didn't want to pay Adele any money either. In reality, I did not like Mrs. Laurent. She scared me, and the thought of never having to see her again kind of made me happy. But, Johnsons weren't quitters, so I couldn't just drop out. Not only that, Mrs. Laurent's cat just had five kittens, and I wanted to be able to play with them and watch them grow. So I was left with one option: I had to learn how to read music.

And so, I did. It was really simple – all that worrying over nothing. If someone had only told me before how easy it was to play if you just understood what those little black dots were all about, well then maybe I would have tried to learn to read music right from the beginning.

22

I was playing Pachelbel's Canon in D as fast as my fingers could move, somehow thinking that the quicker I played, the sooner my thirty minutes would be over. It wasn't working. When I came to the end of the page, I leaned way back on the piano bench in order to see the timer on the back of the kitchen stove – seventeen more minutes to go. I kept on leaning all the way back until my head was resting upside down on the floor. All the blood flowed to my head in a rush. Whew, I loved that feeling. I sat up quickly and closed my eyes, letting the blood drain back out of my face.

"Lizzie," I said, "are we alone?" Lizzie was sitting on the couch, reading, waiting for me to finish practicing.

"I think so," she replied, looking around.

"Good." I carefully stood up and made my way into the kitchen. "I never do this normally," I said over my shoulder to Lizzie, "but today is different." When I reached the stove, I turned the timer until there were only two minutes left. I then dashed over to the piano and started practicing my scales. By the time my fingers had run up two octaves and back down again four separate times, the buzzer went off.

"I'm done!" I yelled as I headed outside to see if Uncle Roy was still there. Lizzie dog-eared the page that she was on, threw her book onto the couch, and quickly followed me. We found him standing by his car with another policeman, deep in conversation. They didn't notice us, so I motioned for Lizzie to be quiet and follow me as I slipped over to one of my favorite trees in the yard and pulled myself up onto the lowest branch.

I really did love that tree. The limbs naturally lined up like monkey bars, and I would swing from one branch to another. One day, not too long before Lizzie arrived in Seattle, I was playing on it and I got an idea. Somehow, I wanted to let the whole world know what an extraordinary tree I had in my front yard. Earlier that day, Scottie and I had been playing in the basement, and we found a pile of scrap wood. We spent about an hour deciding what we could build with it. Scottie got bored and wandered away before we came up with a plan, so I lost interest too.

Later that day, it occurred to me, as I was swinging on the branches, that we could use some of the scrap wood to make a sign for the tree. All of us kids, but especially Scottie and I, spent hours playing in it, so I thought it deserved its own sign. I couldn't find Scottie, so I went and found a small can of paint in our craft box and got one of the biggest pieces of wood out of the pile. I painted the words "The Best Climbing Tree in Washington" on it in bright red. Then, I got my dad's favorite hammer and some nails and, after it dried, I nailed the sign right into the trunk of the tree. I was standing back, admiring my work, when Scottie came around the corner of the house.

"What're you doing?" he asked me.

"I just thought we needed to, you know, honor this tree." I said to him, pointing to my sign. Except for the fact that it was a little bit crooked, it looked pretty good. Scottie was holding two STP racers in his hands, so I knew that he wanted me to play with him. He stared at the tree for a minute, kind of nodding his head.

"I like it," he said. "Wanna play?"

"Sure," I replied. I wanted to give him a big hug, but I knew better. Getting his approval was a rare thing; I didn't want to ruin the moment by getting mushy on him. I took the purple racer out of his hand and followed him into the back yard.

❧ ❧

Lizzie and I were clinging to the higher branches of our tree, listening to Uncle Roy and the other officer discuss the details of his arrangement with the man who had called earlier that day.

"This is the way it's going to be," he was saying. "I'm meeting the guy near the Space Needle at ten o'clock tomorrow morning. We're actually meeting on the corner of Broad Street and Fourth Avenue North. There's a phone booth there."

"And you're bringing how much money?"

"Well, I've been talking to the chief on and off all day. He is going to supply me with ten-thousand dollars in counterfeit money – no way will this guy be able to tell it's not real. I'm going to put it in a briefcase. I'll be wearing jeans and a white shirt. When I get to the corner at ten, he's supposed to call me at that phone booth. He'll give me further instructions then."

"But what about the girl? Did he tell you he was going to have the girl with him?"

"He hung up before we even got to the girl. Presumably, he will have her with him, and that is what we will be discussing on the phone tomorrow. I've been instructed not to let go of the briefcase until I've got the girl in my sight – even better, in my grasp."

"I don't know, Roy. This seems too simple. Do you really think this guy nabbed a girl from a middle class family for the money?"

"I know. That's bothering me too. If you're going to go for ransom, then grab some rich kid, right?" Uncle Roy said, shaking his head. "Let's just hope that he's a druggie with a habit to support, who acted before he thought things through."

"Who's your backup?" the policeman asked Uncle Roy.

"There will be a team of plainclothesmen who will get there before the sun comes up. The plan is that they will carefully encircle us as we are making our transaction. Our goal is to end up with the girl, healthy and alive, and with the perpetrator in cuffs."

"Sounds good. I wish you the best, Man." The officers shook hands. Uncle Roy said something under his breath and the other policeman laughed. They split up then, Uncle Roy heading back in to my house, and the other policeman getting into his car and driving away. We scooted down the tree so fast that I accidentally caught the hem of my shorts on a branch. I could hear the popping of my seam as I quickly yanked the cloth out of the clutch of the tree.

"Oh, boy – Mom is going to love this," I said, looking at Lizzie as I showed her the ripped material, poking my finger through the hole. I really needed to learn how to sew. We caught up with Uncle Roy as he went to talk to my parents, who were sitting in the living room, drinking coffee. My mom immediately jumped up to get a cup for Roy.

"Cream and sugar?" she asked, as she walked into the kitchen.

"Thanks, that'll be fine," Uncle Roy replied. I walked over to my dad and crawled into his lap. Lizzie sat on the floor right next to us.

"How're you doing, Princess?" my dad asked me. His breath smelled like coffee. It was a nice smell.

"I'm good," I said. "How're you?" I already knew the answer, but I asked anyway. My dad absent-mindedly patted my knee with his free hand. It kind of tickled, but I refrained from giggling. I knew that this was not the time.

"Well, Honey, I've been better," he replied. I wished that I could have said something to my dad to make him feel better. But he seemed to disappear into his own thoughts until my mom came back into the room and handed Roy his cup of coffee. He took a sip and nodded.

"Mmm. This hits the spot, Mrs. Johnson."

"I hope it's not burnt," my mom apologized as she made her way back to her chair.

"It's just perfect, thank you," he replied, looking at my dad. "Now, are we all clear on what's going to be happening tomorrow?" he asked.

"Yes, Roy, I think we understand. And it will be okay if we are down there waiting in some hidden spot?"

"Yes, Sir," Uncle Roy replied, "we are hoping that we will be able to safely escort your daughter right into your waiting arms tomorrow morning."

"Can I come, too?" I asked my father. But he must not have heard me, because he just kept talking with Uncle Roy. Finally, I got out of his lap, and Lizzie and I left the room.

I could hardly sleep that night. Every detail of the policemen's conversation kept playing and replaying in my head. I would have liked to have believed that this bad guy had randomly grabbed Angela off the street, hidden her away for a couple of weeks while he got all the information he needed to contact our family, and then made his play for money in exchange for the girl. I'd seen shows like that on television, and they always had a happily-ever-after ending. I would have liked to have believed that, but something deep inside just wouldn't let me accept that it could be so easy.

I tossed and turned all night. There were no windows in our little added-on room. The original owners built the room to be their pantry, a place to put oversized pots and pans, and jars of canned berries and fruit, right off the kitchen, but it was a perfect room for Scottie and Lizzie and me. And it was a perfect place for my dad to study. The only thing was that you couldn't tell what time of the day it was. I never knew whether the sun was up or if it was still moon-time.

When the sun finally did rise and I could hear movement and voices in the house, I quickly got out of bed and got dressed. I figured that I would go downtown with my parents and hide away with them until they brought Angela to us. There was no way that I was not going to be there when they found Angela. I must have been preoccupied that morning, because I was startled when Lizzie came up next to me and tapped my arm.

"Oh, Lizzie. You scared me!" I said to her.

"Sorry, Bobbi," she said. "So, are we going to be allowed to go with your parents?" I looked at my friend Lizzie. For the first time that summer I wished that she would just stay and play with Scottie. I knew that I would be pushing it just to get a place for one kid in the police car that morning, let alone two. But something about the way she looked at me, with total trust, like she never had any question about whether or not I would include her in the morning's events, made me feel real bad. How could I even think of leaving Lizzie behind? Would Joe leave Frank just when they were about to solve the mystery? I don't think so.

"Oh, yeah, I'm not sure yet," I said to Lizzie. "I'm just about to ask my mom." She nodded and smiled. She believed in me. I had to kind of swallow because I had gotten a big lump in my throat. My mother was in the kitchen.

"Mom, I know that you are going to be in a police car and everything, and that you and Daddy are going to be worried and nervous and all – but I was wondering, do you think that Lizzie and I could come downtown with you?" My mom looked at me, but it was like she didn't see me at all.

"Ask your father," she said. She went over to the percolator and started to make coffee. I looked at Lizzie and shrugged.

"Well that was better than no, I guess," I whispered into Lizzie's ear. I couldn't find my dad, so we never really got permission to go in the car with my parents, but nobody seemed to notice when we climbed in after them. Both Lizzie and I seemed to know, without having talked about it to each other beforehand, that it would be in our best interest that morning to bring as little attention to ourselves as possible. And so, we sat stiff and quiet in the back of the unmarked car, with my parents sitting on either side of us.

The car was a navy blue sedan – a brand new Ford Custom 500. It was the kind of car that bounces up and down with every pothole. I closed my eyes and breathed through my nose. For some reason, the only car that I could ride in that didn't make me sick to my stomach was our old reliable station wagon. I didn't want to get sick that morning. The last time I rode in a sedan, it was my grandpa's. His was a white Chevy Impala that had been given to him by the people in his church because he worked for no salary. My grandpa was a preacher – twice on Sundays and every Wednesday evening – and he laid asphalt on Mondays through Fridays to pay the bills. He and my grandma lived in Yakima, Washington. Their house was located on the grounds of a National Forest.

Yakima is in the middle of Washington, right where the Yakima River and the Naches River join together. I loved the Yakima River. I had seen a bunch of rivers when we went on vacations across the United States, but not one of those rivers was as fast as the Yakima. Every time we visited, the first thing my grandpa would do was take us out back to see the river. It ran right through their back yard. It was so loud that we had to yell to each other in order to be heard. When our visits lasted over the weekend, we would go with my grandparents to their church, which was a long way from their home, up in the foothills of the Cascades. We kids would always ask to drive with my grandpa and my grandma because we didn't get to see them very often.

After about five minutes of being in their bouncy sedan, I would always start to get that feeling; a feeling that – I don't care what my mother said – wouldn't go away by staring straight ahead, or closing my eyes, or thinking about something else. Inevitably, I would have to crawl over someone so I could get close to the window. Sometimes, taking deep, gulping breaths of the fresh air would help me feel better. More often than not, my grandpa would have to pull the car over so that I could get out and throw up.

I had that feeling now, sitting in between my mom and dad. I glanced over at Lizzie to see if she was feeling it too. But Lizzie was not only not getting car sick, she was reading – something that I had never, ever been able to do in a car. I quickly closed my eyes because just watching her read made me feel sicker. When we finally arrived downtown, the police officer who was driving the car said that we could get out and walk around for a bit. He had made eye contact with me through the rear-view mirror a couple of times on the drive down, and I think maybe he had noticed the cold sweat that was breaking out on my brow. He was probably thinking, 'Get this kid out of my squad car'.

It was early, five o'clock in the morning. We weren't all that close to the Space Needle, but it was so tall that we still had a great view of the top. Lizzie was impressed.

"Wow," she exclaimed, "it looks like a giant flying saucer!"

"I know," I said, "Isn't it cool?" I had been drawn to the Space Needle since the first time my dad had taken us to look at it. "And guess what? There's a restaurant up there that turns around and around so you can see the whole State of Washington!"

"Really?" Lizzie's eyes grew wide. "I wish we could go up there." I had been wishing that we could go up there for as long as we had been in Seattle, but it cost fifty cents a person just to go to the observation deck. And who knew how much it would cost to actually go to the restaurant? There was no way that we would be able to go. After all, as my mom always said, we weren't made of money.

"Yeah, me too," I sighed. "Maybe when we get Angela back, my dad will let us celebrate by taking us up to the observation deck."

"He would never leave the other kids out, though," Lizzie replied. I looked at her and smiled. She was no longer the homesick little visitor. She had really made herself one of the family over the past few weeks.

"No, you're right. He wouldn't," I said. The policemen took us to the stationhouse so that we would be more comfortable while we waited. He pointed to a coffee percolator near one of the desks.

"Help yourself," he said, and then added, "at your own risk." He looked at Lizzie and me and winked. I felt my face growing hot and quickly looked away. Why did everything make me blush nowadays? It made me so mad. I had always been a friendly person, a person who loved to meet new people. At school, I was the kid who loved to participate in class. My hand would shoot up when a teacher asked a question, and I would secretly be thrilled when she called on me. But this year, I would still instinctively raise my hand when I knew an answer to a question, but when the teacher would say my name, I would start to blush. Then, because I was so embarrassed that I was blushing, I would stumble all over my words until the teacher would finally have to call on somebody else. It was humiliating.

"Would you like some coffee, Honey?" my dad asked my mother.

"Sure – that would be nice. Thank you, Daddy," my mom replied.

For as long as I could remember, my mom had called my dad 'Daddy'. Sometimes my friends would point that out to me like it was weird, but it would have sounded strange to have heard my mom calling my dad Daniel. Daniel? My dad was definitely not a Daniel, or even a Danny or a Dan. He was Daddy.

It was ten o'clock and at that very moment the telephone on the corner of Broad Street and Fourth Avenue North should have been ringing. My dad had gotten the four of us to hold hands.

"Dear Heavenly Father," he prayed, "we come to you right now asking that you would provide a miracle. We pray that you would keep Roy and all of the other policemen safe as they bring our Angela back to us quickly. We pray that you would calm all of our nerves, especially Angela's, and that in a few minutes, we will be able to hold her in our arms again. We know that greater is He that is within us than he that is within the world. You are a good God. Amen."

I had always loved the way my dad talked to God, like he was just picking up a conversation that had been dropped a few minutes earlier. Even when things were bad, like when my parents were worrying about money, or someone was sick or – worst of all – when Angela had gone missing, my dad would still include in his prayers, 'You are a good God'. I didn't quite understand how he could say that. It didn't feel like God was a good God, but I was glad that my dad believed it was true – because he believed, I believed.

We could hear Uncle Roy talking on the police radio. "It's half past the hour and the phone has not rung yet," he reported. The policemen told us that Uncle Roy had been hooked up with one of those walkie-talkies that was pinned to his shirt. All he had to do was hide his mouth by pretending to cough or yawn and he could talk without looking like he was talking because he wasn't holding a radio in his hand. The two policemen who were on our end were pacing back and forth in the cramped office. The four of us wanted to pace, but there wasn't enough room. Instead, we each found our own way to cope with our nerves.

Daddy was sitting on the edge of his seat, leaning forward with his eyes shut, probably continuing his conversation with God. My mom was lying back in her chair, resting her head against the wall behind it. Her eyes were also closed, and I knew that she was praying too. Lizzie was sitting Indian-style on the floor, rocking slightly as she read her book. I wished that I had brought a book, but I hadn't, so I sat on the floor next to Lizzie with my legs stretched out in front of me, and tried my hardest to pray. I did really well at first, but then my eyes caught sight of the hair on my legs. Oh, how I hated it! I wished that my mom would let me shave my legs. We weren't allowed to wear pants to school, and all the cool girls were wearing anklets. Their moms let them shave their legs. I was stuck wearing knee socks. At least they covered up the hairiest part of my legs. I looked at the clock on the wall – I needed to start praying again – but, even as I was trying to ask the Lord to get Angela back for us safe and sound, all I could think about was how much I wished that my mom would let me shave my legs.

By eleven o'clock the policemen were really restless.

"What do you think?" I could hear them whispering to each other, trying not to let us hear them.

"Maybe it was just a prank call," the policeman named Andy said.

"I'm afraid that's what I'm beginning to think," the other officer whispered.

"The chief says to give it another hour. In case the guy is just nervous."

"Yeah – well, let's hope he finds his nerve."

I was starting to get a sick feeling in my stomach, almost like I felt in the car earlier. We were not going to get Angela back today. I knew it. I just knew it. By noon, operation 'Save Angela' was officially called off. Uncle Roy showed up at the office a few minutes later. He walked over to my parents and stuck his hand out to my dad to shake it.

"I'm awfully sorry, folks," he said as my dad returned his handshake. "There's always a chance with these phone calls that they'll turn out to be false alarms. But we have to take them seriously."

"Roy," my dad replied, "we understand. We most certainly understand, and we appreciate all that you have done for us today. I'm sorry it was just a waste of time." Uncle Roy balled his hand into a fist and pounded it into his other hand.

"Yeah, me too. I was really hoping..."

"Well, what do we do next?" my father broke in.

"I'll let you know as soon as I know, how's that?" Uncle Roy replied. "We've still got people manning your phones and, who knows, maybe they'll have gotten a lead while we were down here this morning." Uncle Roy looked over at the policeman who was walking toward us. "Okay, here's Phil. He'll drive you home now. I'll be dropping by later to brief you on the steps we'll be taking next." Uncle Roy put his hand back out and he and my dad shook on it.

"Okay. Thank you, Roy."

Phil ushered us out to the sidewalk. "Hey, Bobbi," he said, looking at me. "Would you like to sit up front?" Would I like that? Wow, more than Christmas!

"Yes, Sir," I mumbled, as my cheeks once again grew warm and flushed. "Can Lizzie sit up front too?"

23

When we got home, we found the rest of the family waiting for us in the living room. Graham had been in charge, and he had not let either Adele or Scottie out of his sight. Poor Graham, he had been racked with guilt ever since Angela disappeared. When they heard the kitchen door open, all three of them pounced on us in gleeful anticipation. It was an excruciatingly sad moment for all of us. Adele burst out crying when she realized that Angela was not with us, and she ran to hide herself in the room that she and Angela had spent so much time in together. Graham stared at us, or really, at my dad, like he was hoping that Daddy would eventually crack a smile and pull Angela out of a hat or something. And little Scottie slumped over dejectedly and wandered off, to who-knows-where to do who-knows-what.

All I wanted to do was to go to my room with Lizzie and read. I needed to go to some far away place and forget all about the sad reality of the entire day, but just as I was about to open the door, the phone rang. The policeman in charge at the moment was the one to answer the phone.

He talked for a minute and then said, "Is there a Bobby here?"

I looked at him and replied, "Yeah, I'm right here."

"You're Bobby?" he said to me as he extended his hand and gave me the receiver. I nodded and put the phone to my ear, too tired to recite my usual explanation about having a boy's name.

"Hello?" I really couldn't imagine who it could be. "Oh, hi." It was Mrs. Anderson. She wanted to know if I could take care of Nicky that evening.

"Would you mind if my friend Lizzie came with me?" I asked her. I didn't mind babysitting, but I didn't want to leave Lizzie alone. Mrs. Anderson assured me that Lizzie was welcome. I found Lizzie in our room, sitting on her bed.

"Do you care if we babysit Nicky tonight, Lizzie?" I asked her, scrunching my face up like, I hope you don't mind, because I already said yes. But Lizzie was true to form.

"No, I don't mind," she replied. "Sounds like fun." I smiled at her.

"Thanks, I'll split the money with you." Lizzie just smiled. We were both tired, too tired to talk or to read – so we put a record on the record player. It was *The Prince and the Pauper*, one of my favorites. Strangely, I had always related to the Prince over the years that I had been listening to that record. How exciting it would be, I thought, to become a completely different person who nobody recognized. Oh, the freedom, I thought, the lovely freedom. Living the life of a prince didn't appeal to me because he had such a strict schedule. If there was anything I valued, it was my free time to play.

We listened to records for about thirty minutes, and then my mom called us in to eat dinner. Lizzie and I had not really eaten anything that entire day. I don't think we even realized it until we went in to the kitchen and smelled the food. Somehow, in just one half hour, my mom managed to whip up spaghetti with meat sauce, a salad, and garlic bread. It smelled so good that I thought I was going to die if I couldn't eat in the next second.

We ate in the kitchen when we lived in Seattle. There really wasn't any formal dining room in our house. But the kitchen was always warm and comfortable. Our table was kind of like a booth in a restaurant. On one side, there was one long chair that was built in to the wall and it curved around the side of the table. On the other side was a long bench. Eight people could easily fit at our table. We left Angela's spot empty, and our mother still set a plate for her at every meal. At first we kids thought it was strange, but after a while it became a symbol of our unwavering hope. We were going to find our number eight.

I was sad after our disappointing day, but also, I was mad. I felt desperate to go and find Angela even if it was the last thing that I ever did. Lizzie and I crossed the street to babysit at five minutes before six. My mom had always emphasized to me the importance of being just a little bit early. I was glad Lizzie was with me, because the first person we saw when we got to the house was Mr. Anderson. Ever since I had found that room in the basement of his house, I had been a little – no, a lot – afraid of Mr. Anderson. How could someone look so normal, and yet have such a disgusting secret? It was a relief when Mrs. Anderson came out of her bedroom to tell us what their plans were for the evening.

"We are going out with friends to a very nice restaurant downtown," she said. Her face was all happy with anticipation. "We expect to be home by nine. Well, we might be as late as ten.

Will that be a problem?" I told her that that would not be a problem at all, and that she should go and have a nice dinner. After all, Nicky went to bed at eight-thirty, so really, Lizzie and I would be paid for the last hour and a half for just watching TV. That was cool. The Andersons left and Lizzie and I outdid ourselves. We were better than television at entertaining the little bored boy. We played I-Spy, we played tag, and finally, we played hide-and-go-seek.

At one point, when it was Lizzie's and my turn to hide, and Nicky was counting to fifty, I decided to try and see if the door was locked to Mr. Anderson's secret room. I felt my way over to the shelves in the dark, this time I didn't pull the string to turn the other light on. I pushed on the shelf-door and it moved inward. Goosebumps started to spread all over my body. I don't know why I decided to go in, because it had made me feel so dirty the first time, but for some reason, I just felt compelled to push my way into the secret room one more time.

Once I got into the dimly lit space, I saw that it was pretty much the same as it had been when I had seen it before, but this time I noticed there was a table along one wall that held trays and chemicals. I looked around to see what else he kept in his room. There was a desk on the back wall in the corner, where the glowing lamp sat. I walked over to the desk. It was clear from the pile of mail spread over it that this was the room where Mr. Anderson paid his bills and took care of his business. I wasn't sure exactly what he did for a living, but I knew that he worked downtown. Come to think of it, I believe that I heard that he worked near Pike Place Market.

"I'm up to forty, Bobbi!" I heard Nicky shouting. "Forty-one, forty-two, forty-three..." I was running out of time. I quickly slipped out of the room, pulling the door closed behind me. I heard it click shut. Where could I hide? I noticed a pile of dirty clothes next to the washing machine, and dove into it, pulling sheets and socks over my head. I then tried to quiet my beating heart. It took Nicki forever to find me. When he finally did, I had to wash my face to get the smell of stinky socks out of my nose. When we got Nicky to fall asleep, I motioned for Lizzie to join me in the kitchen, which was on the other side of the house from Nicky's room.

"Lizzie," I said in a whisper, "did I ever tell you about Mr. Anderson's office?"

"What about his office?" she asked.

"Well, it's hidden behind a secret door, for one thing," I said.

"Cool," Lizzie exclaimed. "Show me."

"Okay," I said, "only I have to warn you: it's gross." As we made our way down the stairs, I filled Lizzie in on Mr. Anderson's choice of wall covering. Lizzie changed her mind about wanting to see the office, but I wanted to show her how the door worked, so she reluctantly followed me down to the basement. When we got to the shelves I pushed on them, but they would not open.

"Oh, man. I wonder if it's locked?" I said. "It just pushed open last time." I bent down to see if there was some kind of doorknob, but I couldn't see anything except a knothole in the wood. For some reason I put my finger on the knot and pushed it. It made a clicking noise, and when I gave it a push, the door leading in to his office opened up.

"Wow, did you see that, Lizzie?" I asked. But Lizzie was staring straight down at the floor. She was holding onto my shirt and waiting for me to lead her into the room. I guess she didn't want to risk seeing any of the pictures on the wall. Once we got to the desk, she tugged on my shirt.

"Can I open my eyes now?" she asked.

"Yes, Lizzie, you can open your eyes." She did, but she still refused to lift her gaze up.

"Why are we in here?" she demanded.

"I know, the pictures are horrible," I said. "But isn't this secret room neat? I wish we could find one like it in our house."

"Hey," Lizzie interrupted me. "Mr. Anderson must've taken Nicky to that underground city tour that you were telling me about."

"What?" I asked. "Why would you say that, Lizzie?"

"See?" she said, pointing to a ticket stub on the desk. "This is for the underground tour at Pioneer Square. Isn't that what you were telling me about the other day?"

"Yes, it is. I wonder when they went?" I said. "This is exactly what I was telling you about the other day, Lizzie. We'll have to ask Nicky about it. You know I wanted to take you there before, well, you know... Lizzie suddenly grabbed my arm tightly.

"What?" I asked her. "You're hurting me!" But Lizzie didn't loosen her grip. She was looking up like she had heard something. I stopped talking and started to listen. Sure enough, there was a creaking of the floorboards right over our heads. I looked at my watch, which had glow-in-the-dark hands. It was eight-fifty. "They're early," I whispered.

"Let's get out of here," Lizzie replied hoarsely. We quickly made our way out of the room, pulling the door shut behind us.

"The laundry," Lizzie said quietly.

"We can't hide, Lizzie," I said, as I ran after her to the pile of clothes.

"We're not going to hide, Silly, we're going to do it," she said. And she opened the washing machine lid as if she knew exactly what she was doing. I personally had never washed an article of clothing in my life. That and cooking were the two chores that my mother would never let any of us kids do.

"Okay," Lizzie said loudly in a sing-song voice, "we'll start with the whites." I looked at her and shrugged.

"That's right, Bobbi, put all the white clothes in the washing machine so that we can wash them." Lizzie was giving me a look, and I realized that I had better start playing along with her. I started stuffing everything white into the washing machine, as Lizzie scooped some detergent and started to pour it on top of the clothes.

"Okay, Lizzie," I said loudly, "here's the last white towel." We heard the basement door open and then Mr. Anderson called down to us.

"Hey, are you girls down there?"

"Oh, Mr. Anderson," I said as if I was surprised to hear his voice. "Yes, we're down here doing your laundry." We heard a shuffling of footsteps, and then Mrs. Anderson spoke up.

"You girls are doing our laundry! Oh, my goodness. You are such angels!" I looked at Lizzie and gave her a quick smile. That was really fast thinking on her part.

"You girls really didn't need to do this," Mrs. Anderson said, as she walked into the laundry area. "But thank you so much! It gets so tiresome doing all the chores around the house, you know?"

"Anytime, Mrs. Anderson!" I said. "Lizzie and I aim to please." I knew that I sounded stupid even as I was saying the words, but I was so nervous that I was afraid that I might start giggling, so I just blurted out the first thing that came in to my head.

We got paid two dollars for our three hours. They usually only paid fifty cents an hour, so we felt lucky. Mr. Anderson volunteered to walk us across the street.

"Oh no, we're fine," I said for both Lizzie and myself. But then I gave him a big smile. "Thanks so much for offering. You two have a nice evening now." Lizzie and I waved and smiled our way out the door. I didn't feel safe until we were in our house and I had shut and locked our bedroom door.

"That was scary!" Lizzie said as soon as we were safely seated next to each other on top of my bunk bed.

"It *was* scary!" I said. "You don't think he could tell that I was acting weird, do you?"

"Weirder than you were when we got there and you were answering his questions but looking at the dog? No, I just think that he thinks you're weird."

"Thanks a lot, Lizzie," I laughed, and I threw my pillow at her.

"But now I know why he freaks you out. Why didn't you tell me about that dungeon with all the nasty pictures before?"

"Because, I was trying to forget that I knew about it," I said, screwing my face up in disgust.

"Do you think that Nicky and his mom know about that room?" Lizzie asked, making a face back at me.

"I don't know," I said. It didn't seem possible that Mrs. Anderson could know about the room and act the way she did. She was the type of wife and mom who called Nicky and Mr. Anderson 'the two men in my life'. She always fussed over them in one way or another, and they liked to be fussed over. It was embarrassing sometimes. Mr. Anderson and Nicky were both pretty spoiled. I'd always thought that Mrs. Anderson was gaga over her husband, but maybe she knew about his room, and maybe she was afraid that he didn't love her anymore, and so that's why she was so mushy all the time. I thought about my parents. There was no fear in their marriage – only trust. That's the kind of marriage I wanted. I leaned against Lizzie.

"Hey," I said. "Promise me that if you ever find out anything horrible about your husband, you will come and live with me. Okay?" Lizzie laughingly promised.

"But what could be so bad about Scottie?" she said.

"Ohhhh!" I said in a sing-song voice. This was the first time that I had ever heard Lizzie admit that she liked Scottie, even though I always knew it. "Actually," I said, "I am probably the wrong person to ask that question – I have a list."

Lizzie pushed me with her shoulder, but we both broke out laughing. It felt good to goof around for a minute, almost like we were just regular girls with nothing more on our minds than who we liked or what we wanted to watch on TV. We sat quietly together, heads against the wall.

"He sure had a lot of junk on his desk," Lizzie said, out of the blue.

"What desk?" I asked, thinking that she was still talking about Scottie.

"You know," she replied, "the desk in that room."

"Oh," I said. "Yeah, he did." My mind returned to the clutter on Mr. Anderson's desk. "So, they went to the underground city," I said. "I wonder why Nicky didn't tell us about it."

"Yeah," Lizzie agreed, "he always brags about everything." I laughed. She already had Nicky figured out.

"I know. Sometimes he can be a brat," I said. "Did you notice the date on that ticket stub?" I asked Lizzie.

"Uh-uh," she replied. "Why?"

"Oh, I don't know. I just wonder when they went – it had to be pretty recently, otherwise, why would he still have the ticket?" Lizzie nodded her head. "Know what?" I continued, "I think I'm going to sneak back in there and take a look at that stub."

"Why?" Lizzie asked. "Who cares?"

"I'm just curious," I said. "It's just so strange that Nicky hasn't mentioned it."

"I know – but you couldn't pay me to go back into that creepy office," Lizzie said, and her whole body shuddered. I nodded and I started to climb down from the bed.

"Let's go find Scottie and see what he thinks."

"Okay," Lizzie replied. "Where is he, anyway?"

We found him working on a model car at the kitchen table. A couple of policemen were sitting at the table with him. Scottie had already put all the pieces of the car together, and was now carefully painting a lightning bolt on the hood.

"Wow, that looks really good, Scottie," Lizzie cooed. He gave her a quick look and smiled.

"I know. It's a Firefighter Mustang II, Pro-Stocker."

"Cool," Lizzie said.

"How long is it gonna take you?" I asked him, looking at my watch. It was a Charlie-the-Tuna wristwatch. I'd gotten it by sending in ten tuna labels and twenty-five cents for shipping and handling. It was the one possession that I had been able to show off to Nicky that summer.

"I'm almost done," Scottie replied. I could tell he wanted us to leave him alone. Scottie had never been able to do two things at the same time. When he started something, he did not like to be interrupted.

"Okay," I said, "meet us in five minutes in the bedroom. It's really important." I didn't want to talk about what I was planning to do in front of the policemen. I wished that Scottie would look up from his model and catch my eye. I wanted to give him our secret signal.

When we were younger, we had come up with a blinking code that we would send across the table to each other when our dad was reading the devotional after dinner. Closing both eyes two times meant 'Meet me in the back yard as soon as Daddy is finished, and fast before Mom can give us a cleaning-up chore'. Winking with one eye and then the other eye meant 'Go to the carport; we're going to go bike riding' – and a constant winking and blinking of both eyes meant 'I wish he'd hurry up and finish – I gotta get out of here!'

That was the message that I wanted to send him right that minute. With all the policemen hanging around, I didn't want to actually say anything and make them suspicious. But Scottie was lost in his own little world, and there was no talking to him when he went there.

24

"I think we need to go check it out tonight," I was saying to Lizzie when Scottie finally joined us.

"What're you talking about?" Scottie asked, as he pulled himself up to the top bunk to sit with us. Lizzie and I filled him in on the secret room behind the shelves in the Anderson's basement, and then we told him about the naked girl pictures and about finding the ticket stub.

"I want to go back there to see the date on that ticket," I told him.

"Who cares about an old ticket stub?" Scottie asked me.

"I do, okay?" I replied sharply, and then immediately felt bad. I knew I shouldn't get mad at Scottie, but I didn't even know myself why I felt so strongly about getting back into Mr. Anderson's office again. I could hardly explain it to him.

"I don't get it," he pushed further. "I mean, I know that Mr. Anderson is going to get in a lot of trouble for having all those pictures of naked girls. But why do you care about some field trip that he took with Nicky?" I didn't say a thing. My mind started to race. Naked girls. Suddenly I remembered all the clothes that Scottie and I had found in the woods. And then I thought about the chemicals in Mr. Anderson's office. They looked like the same chemicals that Graham used to develop pictures. Could it be possible that Mr. Anderson was going to those woods and getting girls to remove their clothes so he could take pictures of them? I decided not to say anything right then to Scottie and Lizzie.

"You know what?" I finally said. "I'm not really sure if those pictures are photographs or pages from a magazine." I moved to the edge of the bed. "All the more reason to check out that room tonight," I said, as I slid down to the floor.

"Why?" they both asked.

"Because," I replied, "Scottie's right. Mr. Anderson is not supposed to have pictures of naked girls."

"Wait a minute," Scottie said. "I thought you wanted to go look at that ticket stub."

"Yeah, well, I do. And now, I want to take a closer look at those pictures, too," I said, as I walked over to my dresser.

"Bobbi," Scottie said, "you're acting kind of crazy." I turned around and looked at him. And then I started to cry.

"Leave me alone, Scottie. I just have to do this," I said. I knew that I wasn't making any sense, but it didn't matter to me. Earlier that day, when I was sitting in the police car, I had hoped so hard that we were going to get all our questions about Angela's disappearance answered. Instead, we came home without Angela, and with no answers. I knew that Mr. Anderson's secret room had nothing to do with Angela, but there was something mysterious about it, and I desperately needed to solve a mystery.

"Okay," Scottie sighed. "But you're not going to do it without us."

"Yeah," Lizzie agreed.

"Really?" I asked them, and they both nodded their heads. It was all I could do not to start crying again.

&⪪ ⪫

Scottie turned out to be a wealth of knowledge when it came to breaking into our neighbor's house.

"You could just use the basement door out back," he said. "They never lock it." I looked at Scottie.

"How do you know they never lock their door?" I asked him.

"Because," he said, "that's where they keep the dog food. You know, when Graham and I take care of Baxter when they go on vacation."

"Oh," I said. "But they probably only leave that door open when they're gone, don't you think?"

Scottie just shrugged. "I guess there's only one way to find out," he said. I could tell that he was getting excited about our plans for the evening.

"I guess so," I said. "We need to all put dark clothes on, so we blend into the night." Each of us found a dark top and dark pants. Lizzie and I changed on the top bunk, while Scottie changed below us. Once we were ready, we went outside.

"Okay, You Guys," I whispered, "I'll run across the street and try the back door to see if it's unlocked."

"No way," Scottie said. "Baxter will bark like crazy if you just barge in on him. We need to all go together and make sure that Baxter knows it's us. Lizzie and I will distract him, while you go in the house." I didn't tell him so, but I was pretty impressed with Scottie's sleuthing skills.

"Okay," I said. "Let's go." Once we got into their back yard, we all petted Baxter, who was thrilled to have playmates so late at night. And then I walked over to the basement door and turned the knob – it opened. Scottie followed me in and got some food for Baxter. He took it outside while I went deeper into the basement. I had never come into the basement from this direction so I wasn't exactly sure where I was. I walked inch by inch with one arm out in front of me and the other arm feeling along the wall. I began to smell the scent of laundry detergent, so I knew that I must be right by the washing machine. I let go of the wall so that I could walk over to the hall that led off of the laundry area and something brushed my face. Somehow, I managed not to scream. It was just the light string. I stood still and waited for my heartbeat to slow down. Something banged and there was a crash, and then I felt Baxter rubbing up against my leg.

"Baxter. Go, Boy. Go back to Scottie," I whispered. He didn't obey me, and I thought I heard floorboards creaking upstairs. I carefully kept going in the same direction. The other light string hit my face and I hurried to the back of the hall. When I bumped into the shelves, I pushed on them to open the door, but it would not budge! Oh, great – how was I going to find that knothole in the dark? I could now definitely hear creaks coming from upstairs. Maybe they were just turning over in bed? That's what I was hoping. I put my hand underneath what I thought was the right shelf and I started to push on the wall, feeling for the knothole. Nothing. I reached under the next lower shelf and did the same thing. I tried to see in the dark, but it was impossible. Finally, my fingers brushed over something that felt rough and I pushed on it. It didn't budge. I pushed again, this time right in the middle of the rough area and – click – I had found it, and the entire bookshelf shifted inward. I pushed gently on the door to open it wide enough to get in. Baxter was still with me, his tail was wagging and it kept hitting the back of my legs. There was nothing for me to do but to let him in the room with me.

"I think I hear something downstairs," a muffled voice said. It was Mr. Anderson. I could hear him through the floorboards. He sounded like he was directly above me. I hurriedly pushed my way past the open bookshelf and rushed into the room. I looked around at all the walls. They were completely covered with pictures. I could hear footsteps walking around upstairs now.

"Did you leave the dog in?" I vaguely heard a muffled response, but could not make out the words. "Shut up! I don't want to hear your excuses. I'm just gonna go and see." I scanned the first wall. All I could see were pictures from magazines. I tried to see the back wall, but it was harder to see because the light on the desk was not very bright, and the entire wall was in the shadows. I could hear Mr. Anderson stomping across the house, heading toward the stairs. I knew I didn't have any time left. I quickly turned to the last wall. There were pictures from magazines thumb-tacked all over this wall too. On a whim, I reached out and lifted up one of these pictures and there, underneath the magazine page, was a photograph. I quickly pulled the thumb-tack out and grabbed the photo. I then pushed the tack back in to hold the page from the magazine. I looked under another magazine page and saw another photo, and then another and another. Clearly, Mr. Anderson had his own collection of pictures that he had taken himself.

"Baxter, are you down there, Boy?" It was Mr. Anderson and he sounded as if he was at the top of the stairs. I ran to the door and then got out of the room. I pushed it shut, making sure that Baxter had gotten out with me. I could hear footsteps coming down the stairs. I was paralyzed.

"Baxter – that you, Boy?" Mr. Anderson was now downstairs. He was probably making his way to the laundry area. Baxter gave a little bark, and then he rushed away from me toward Mr. Anderson. "Baxter, Boy, did she forget to put you outside?" I was crouched in the corner of the hall. I wondered where Scottie and Lizzie were. I hoped that they were hidden in the shadows outside.

"Out you go, Boy. Hey, there – what are you doing, Baxter?" Oh, no, was Baxter coming back to get me?

"Baxter, heel. Good boy. What's gotten into you anyway? Now get on out there." I could hear the door slam shut, and then the shuffle of feet as Mr. Anderson made his way back into the basement and pulled the light string. I squeezed my eyes shut.

"What in the world?" I dared not open my eyes. What was I going to say? I should have thought up an excuse for coming down here before I came. "Hey, Shirley!" Mr. Anderson called out angrily to his wife. "The dog knocked over the laundry detergent!" He shook his head and grunted. "Well," he mumbled under his breath, "I'll just let her clean it up in the morning. She's the stupid one who forgot to put the dog out."

He pulled the string to turn off the light, and I could hear his feet shuffling over the concrete floor and then up the creaky wooden steps, and then across the floorboards upstairs. I sighed quietly with relief. I waited until I heard the squeak of the mattress springs as he climbed into bed, and then I stood up and walked as quickly as I could out to my freedom. Once I got outside I looked around to see if I could find Scottie and Lizzie.

"Pssssst," I heard. There they were, hiding behind the trash cans in the back of the house. Baxter was right there with them, wagging his tail for all he was worth.

"Let's get out of here!" I whispered, and the three of us took off, careful to close the latch on the gate so that Baxter couldn't get out. I took the steps up our porch three at a time, and then I threw open the door to our little bedroom.

"Are you okay?" Lizzie panted.

"What do you have in your hand?" Scottie asked. I pretended that I was too out-of-breath to speak and I just shook my head.

I didn't look at the photo that I had taken from the wall of Mr. Anderson's office that night, and I didn't show it to Scottie or Lizzie either. It was late. We were tired. And I didn't have the stomach to look into the sad, sad eyes of the girl who would be looking back at me from inside that photo.

I woke up early the next day and I looked down at Scottie to see if he was still sleeping, then over at Lizzie on her little cot. They were both totally out. I pulled the photograph from under my pillow. It was a little crinkled, but I really hadn't wanted to let it out of my reach. I quickly found my *Hardy Boys* book and took out the small page of stickers that I had been using for a bookmark. I covered up the girl's naked breasts and bottom with three small yellow smiley-face stickers. I then stared at her face to see if she looked familiar. She didn't. The picture was pretty big. It looked just like the kind of paper that Graham used in his dark room.

Graham was really into photography, and his collection of equipment grew with every birthday and Christmas. After he got a photo enlarger, he and my dad had converted a tiny basement closet into a darkroom. Two strings were stretched from wall to wall so Graham could hang his newly developed prints as he pulled them out of the chemical fixer. The picture in my hand was a black and white photo, just like the photos that Graham developed in our basement – only Graham's pictures were of trees and stuff. Mr. Anderson's office was probably also his darkroom. That just made sense. And Mrs. Anderson stayed away because she was afraid of ruining his prints. That had to be the reason that she did not know about her husband's deepest darkest secret.

I had been staring at the girl's face and I hadn't even realized that Scottie had climbed up onto my top bunk. My hand was still covering the stickers that covered the girl's body. I was not about to let Scottie see the naked girl. He looked at her face and shook his head like he didn't recognize her, but then he narrowed his eyes.

"Bobbi, this picture was taken at the Haunted Mansion!" Scottie exclaimed.

"What? Why would you say that?" I asked him, looking at the picture again.

"Look, those are the steps leading upstairs; see that broken handrail thingy?" He was pointing to the spindles that were missing and one of them that was broken in two, but was still hanging from the handrail. "And look," Scottie continued, "there is the doorway leading to the kitchen. See the old refrigerator? And see the hole in the floor right in front of it?" He was right. This picture had been taken in the Haunted Mansion! Scottie and I just looked at each other.

"Wow," I said.

"Remember how we used to always see those hippies hanging out at the Haunted Mansion?" Scottie asked.

"Yeah. I wonder if she was one of them?"

"I don't know," he said.

"So, you think that Mr. Anderson would go and hang out with the hippies?" I asked. Scottie just laughed. "I know," I said, trying to picture Mr. Anderson in a tie-dyed shirt. "That kind of makes me laugh, too." We sat there on my top bunk, leaning back against the wall and trying to put the puzzle together, but it just had too many missing pieces.

"What do you think, Scottie? Should we tell Uncle Roy about all this?"

He nodded. "Yeah, I think we should. I don't know if he'll believe us, but we'll just have to make him."

"Is Lizzie awake yet?" I asked. Scottie leaned over the bed.

"Nope. She's asleep."

"Okay. We'll wait until she wakes up, don't you think?"

"All right. Want to listen to a record?"

"Yeah – how about *20,000 Leagues under the Sea?* I want to go far, far away from here."

25

After the record was over, Scottie and I got restless waiting for Lizzie to wake up, so we went into the living room and turned on the television. We were hoping to watch a cartoon, but the only thing that was on was the news. We just sat there, not really watching, but feeling a bit too lazy to actually turn the TV off. After the weather and the sports there was a special late-breaking report that I am sure both Scottie and I would have ignored had they not mentioned the name of the road that all the reporters were gathered on.

"Scottie," I said, "what are they saying?"

"I'm not sure, but I just heard them mention Highland Terrace Drive."

"Me too," I said. "Turn it up." Scottie reached over to the TV and turned up the volume. We were both sitting on the floor, right in front of it. I'm sure that if my mom had seen us she would have yelled at us to move back because we were going to ruin our eyes and get radiation poisoning. But she was busy doing the laundry or something.

I always thought that it was funny that my mom worried that we kids would get radiation poisoning from sitting too close to the television, because she never seemed to worry that my dad worked at a nuclear power plant. Back then, he was always setting the Geiger counter off – once, he was contaminated so badly that he had to throw out his new jumpsuit.

My mom was not happy. "Honey, you should be more careful," she said. "I sure hope that the company will pay for new coveralls."

I think the reason my mom wasn't too concerned about the radiation that my dad got exposed to out at Hanford was because everyone in Richland made a living at that plant and there was a general trust and belief in nuclear energy that the Hanford families shared.

❧ ❧

"...not the first time that the police have been called to this particular site in Seattle," the reporter was saying. "For a number of months now, the police have found evidence of juvenile pornography being produced in these woods..."

"What does that mean?" Scottie asked. "Juvenile pornography?"

"I don't know. Shhh," I said, waving my hand in his face to silence him. "Let's hear what else they have to say."

"Although they have not found the guilty party or parties, it is clear that these woods have been used as a kind of stage for illicit movies and photography sessions over the past year, at least. An unidentified runaway has just been picked up by the police. She has been missing from her home in Bellevue for two months. Apparently, she made a shelter for herself in these woods, right here in the middle of Seattle. She said that she got the idea from reading the book *My Side of the Mountain* in school."

"Oh, I loved that book," I said.

"Shhh!" Scottie gave me a glare, and then turned back to the newscast.

"Police have found clothing and undergarments in various places throughout these woods. The young girl has stated that the clothing did not belong to her. She did confirm that she and other girls were involved in certain activities with an unidentified man who was wearing a uniform. Police have taken the girl in for questioning, and are trying to learn the identity of the uniformed man. Stay tuned for further updates on this case."

Scottie and I looked at each other. We were thinking the same thing – all those clothes that we had seen when we were in those woods, and the campfire that we had found. Had that been the campfire the girl used to cook on? Had she been watching us from her hidden spot? It sent chills up my spine just thinking about how close we had been to danger. I wondered how old the runaway was, and what had gone so wrong in her life that she would leave her home. I felt sorry for her. Obviously, she liked to read and she must have had a good imagination. We probably would have gotten along really well. I found myself wishing that I had been the one to find her in her carved-out tree – I would have helped her. I would have kept her from that guy in the uniform. If only I'd have known that she was there. I wondered what was going to happen to her now. Scottie stood up, turned off the TV, and looked at me.

"Bobbi," he said, "this might sound crazy, but do you think that Mr. Anderson could be the guy who was taking pictures in the woods?"

"Mr. Anderson? He doesn't wear a uniform."

"Maybe not, but we know he's taken pictures of naked girls in the Haunted Mansion. Maybe he has something to do with the case they're talking about on television."

"Scottie," I said, thinking out loud, "I just thought of something."

"What?" Scottie asked.

"This might be stretching things, but we're pretty sure that Angela walked right by those woods on that day she disappeared. Do you think it's possible that there's a connection?"

"No way – Angela would *never* let him take pictures of her!" Scottie snapped.

"I'm not saying that Angela would let him take pictures of her," I replied. "I'm just saying…"

"Well, don't!" he cut in. Scottie stood up and stomped toward the door.

"Where are you going?" I asked him.

"To see if Lizzie is awake," Scottie replied. "We need to get her up and then go talk to Uncle Roy." I felt like he had misunderstood what I was trying to say, but I didn't try to explain myself – I just followed him into our bedroom. We found Lizzie still fast asleep. I gently touched her on the shoulder.

"Lizzie, wake up," I urged. She rolled over and opened her eyes. Scottie immediately began to tell her what we had seen on the news and what we suspected. Lizzie blinked her eyes. I think she was still mostly asleep. I turned to Scottie.

"I don't think she's heard anything we said."

"Lizzie, are you hungry?" Scottie asked her.

"A little," she croaked.

"Okay," I said, "I'll go get you some breakfast." I went into the kitchen and poured out a bowl of Rice Krispies and then got the blackberries out of the fridge and covered them with sugar. Lizzie came into the kitchen wearing her bathrobe. There were two policemen sitting at our breakfast table, and they nodded to us as we sat down next to them.

"So," I asked them, "what do you think about the runaway girl that they found just down the street?"

"How do you know about that, Kid?"

"I just saw it on the news," I said. I leaned over to Lizzie.

"Don't you hate it when they call you Kid?" I whispered to her. She nodded her head and giggled from behind the large blue cereal box.

"It already made the news?" the other policeman said. "They just discovered that girl a few hours ago."

"Yeah," I said to him. "Are you and Uncle Roy going to be involved in this case?"

"That's police business, Little Girl. Has nothing to do with you." I rolled my eyes at Lizzie and she giggled.

"So, do either of you know where Uncle Roy is?" I asked. The only policeman that didn't think of me as being a two-year-old was Uncle Roy. I really wanted to talk with him.

"Yeah, he's somewhere around here," the one called Jack said. "I need to smoke." He slid out from behind our table and went outside. The other policeman followed him.

"I hate to sound mean, Lizzie," I said to her, "but those cops make me so mad. They think we're just kids!"

"Yeah, I know," Lizzie agreed, looking mildly shocked that I had used the word 'cop'. I knew that I was being disrespectful, but I'd heard other kids call them pigs, which was a lot worse. I let out an exasperated sigh.

"We need to go find your uncle. At least he listens to us," I said. "I told him that someday you and Scottie and I are going to be private investigators and he thought that was great."

"He's nice," Lizzie said.

"Yeah – he *is* nice," I agreed. "When you're finished, let's go find him, okay?"

"Okay. I'm almost done," Lizzie said around a big bite of cereal. She shoved another spoonful into her mouth, and then she ate the last two blackberries. "Yum, that was good," she said. She gave me a toothy grin. "Do I have a purple mouth?" she asked.

I laughed. "Yes, you do. But don't brush your teeth – we don't have time."

I had started to think about the news report again. I could not help but feel like the things that were going on in the woods on

Highland Terrace Drive might have something to do with what had happened to Angela. And so, as Lizzie went to get dressed, I went looking for Uncle Roy. I found him more quickly than I thought I would. He was outside in his squad car. I was feeling anxious, so I decided not to wait for Lizzie and Scottie. I knocked on his window, and asked him if I could get in and talk with him for a minute. He seemed to be a little distracted, but he nodded his head and finished his conversation on his radio.

"Uncle Roy," I said, "I think I might know who that photographer is that they're looking for who was taking pictures of naked girls." Uncle Roy looked at me and smiled. He put his arm on the back of the bench seat and kind of chuckled. I wasn't sure if he was making fun of me or not. He finally spoke.

"You do, huh?"

"Yes, I do," I replied.

"Well, Sweetie, then you would be the first person who has any ideas on this case in the entire state of Washington, but go ahead, shoot." He *was* laughing at me, which made me start to blush, but this time it was more because of frustration than embarrassment.

"Uncle Roy," I said to him, "don't you go acting like all the other cops around here." He looked a little shocked and I have to admit that I was kind of surprised myself at my sudden boldness, but I was tired of being made to feel like I had no brains in my head. I then told him about everything that we'd found at the Anderson's house, and I gave him the photograph that I had taken from Mr. Anderson's secret room.

Something about the way Uncle Roy was looking at me while I was sharing my news with him made me feel uncomfortable. I kept thinking that he was going to start laughing at me again, but Uncle Roy did not laugh. He took the evidence that I gave him, and he looked directly into my eyes. It almost seemed like he was a little bit mad at me. There he sat, in his dark blue police uniform, glaring at me, and, for just a second, as I was staring at a man that I thought I knew, I felt a chill run up my spine. Could it be that the bad guy was sitting in front of me? I suddenly wanted to get my evidence back, but before I could, Uncle Roy reached over and took my hand in his. He shook it real firmly, just like he had done to my dad.

"This is great, Bobbi," he said. "Listen, who else knows about this?"

"Only Lizzie and Scottie and me," I told him.

"Okay, good. I'm going to take this evidence, but I'm going to ask you to keep all of this a secret, okay?" I wasn't sure exactly what he was asking me.

"We wouldn't want to make the SPD look bad now, would we? We'll just keep this to ourselves and I will be sure to get to the bottom of it," Uncle Roy said, and then he patted my knee and gave me a wink. I felt a little uncertain. Uncle Roy had been a friend, but for some reason my whole body tensed up when he patted my knee. I quickly folded my arms across my chest. "Are we clear on this, Bobbi?" he said. He was looking straight into my eyes again. I gave him a nod, and then he said, "Well done, Bobbi, very well done indeed."

26

It was around eleven o'clock in the morning and I felt like I had been kicked in the stomach, but it wasn't because I was hungry. I got out of Uncle Roy's squad car and made my way back to our house and then went to my bedroom. Lizzie was tidying up her little cot.

"Okay, Bobbi. Let's go find my uncle," she said enthusiastically.

"Oh, I already found him," I said, as I sat down on Scottie's lower bunk. I put my face in my hands and rubbed my eyes with my fingers.

"Are you okay?" Lizzie asked me. "What's the matter, Bobbi?" What was I supposed to say? That I suspected that her uncle might be involved in all of this somehow? That maybe he knew something about Angela that he wasn't telling us? I couldn't say that. But that is exactly what I was thinking. What had just happened out there in that squad car? I wasn't really sure. I did know that I felt very stupid – very confused. Who could I trust?

"Lizzie," I said, "Do you think that the photographer in the woods could have been wearing a police uniform?"

"A police uniform? What are you talking about?" Lizzie asked. "Bobbi, policemen are the good guys. When you're in trouble, you go to the police, right?"

"Yes, of course," I replied.

"A policeman would never do anything to harm an American citizen," she stated emphatically.

"No, you sure wouldn't think so," I said feeling guilty that I was even having such thoughts.

"There is no way that the police would do this kind of a crime. What would make you even say such a thing?" Lizzie demanded. When I didn't respond immediately, Lizzie came and sat down next to me. "Bobbi, does Uncle Roy think that it was a police officer?"

"No, he doesn't. Just never mind, Lizzie," I said. "I must be tired."

"So did you talk to my uncle? What did he say?"

"Oh, Lizzie. I don't know exactly. He told me not to worry. I'm sure that he knows what to do…"

"So you told him about Mr. Anderson, then?" Lizzie asked.

"Yes. I told him about Mr. Anderson," I replied.

"And he said?" Lizzie was clearly interested in hearing the details of my conversation with her uncle. And normally I would have recapped every single word, but I just didn't know where to begin. I wasn't sure how to tell her what we had talked about – wasn't sure how to explain that Lizzie's uncle had told me to keep everything hush-hush, almost like he was trying to hide something.

"Oh, Lizzie," I said, "I can't remember what we talked about. All I know is that I no longer have the evidence. Uncle Roy has the photo now, and I am sure that he will use it to find the guy. And now, if it's okay with you, I think I'm going to go take a nap."

And with that I stood and climbed up to my top bunk. This was going to be the first nap that I had ever taken since I was about four years old, but for some reason I was very, very weary. Lizzie was standing on the floor of my room looking up at me. I could tell that I had hurt her, but I couldn't help it. I felt like all I wanted to do was curl into a little ball and disappear. And so I did.

When I woke up, I was slightly discombobulated. What day was it anyway? I wandered into the kitchen to find my mom making dinner, so I realized it was still the same day that I had talked with Uncle Roy. There were no officers in our kitchen, which was unusual.

"Mommy," I asked, "where are the policemen?"

"Well, hello, Sleepyhead," my mom replied. "Yes, isn't it nice? The policemen have finally decided that they don't need to live in our kitchen anymore."

"Oh, really? Why?" I asked, suddenly feeling very awake.

"I'm not really sure, Sweetie. But I have to admit, I wasn't very sorry to see them go." My mom was busy cutting tomatoes into a big green Tupperware salad bowl.

"You think they got a lead or something?" I asked her, trying to sound casual.

"Oh, you know, they never tell me anything, Bobbi," my mom replied. And then she seemed to catch herself. "I mean, don't misunderstand me, I am very grateful for all of their efforts, but it did get tiresome having all those strangers around."

"Yeah, I know," I said. "You had to make a lot of coffee, didn't you?" My mom laughed at that and nodded her head.

"Yes, Bobbi, you're right. I had to make a lot of coffee. It just about wore me out." She laughed again. "If only they had found her – it would have been worth every minute, every cup of coffee…" My mom turned to the stove and began stirring the meat sauce with a wooden spoon. I saw a big tear roll down her cheek. I was sitting at the table where our family ate breakfast, lunch, and dinner – watching my mother prepare yet another meal, while she suffered in silence. It broke my heart.

I closed my eyes and rested my head on the back wall, and tried to make sense of it all. It was at this same table, a few weeks ago, that my dad had been reading from the book of Job to us during our devotional time after dinner, and I couldn't help but feel like we were going through undeserved suffering, just like Job had. There was a point in that story where even his wife told Job to curse God and die. But Job had refused:

Naked I came from my mother's womb,

And naked I will depart.

The Lord gave and the Lord has taken away;

May the name of the Lord be praised.

I had been watching my parents over the last month. At first, they were full of hope, turning to God expectantly. They tried as hard as they could to continue to be happy and positive. After all, they had spent their entire lives being role models for others. They felt responsible for people who were weaker, or less privileged, than they were. They feared that if they faltered in their faith, they would cause other people to falter.

And then they grew tired, but they still remained firm in their faith. With each passing day, their hope of seeing their beautiful daughter again diminished. But, even in the midst of their pain, I saw them trusting in God. It wasn't their faith that was weakening, it was their physical bodies. They recognized that they couldn't keep up their happy front forever, but there was still a peace in their sadness. God had given and He had taken away. They had enjoyed pleasure at His hand; would they now mock Him just because they found themselves in trouble? May it never be so...

But the ordeal had just about worn away their happy front. Strange as it may seem, the more my parents stopped pretending to be happy and brave, the more my respect grew for them. If they could endure what they were going through – and still find peace and comfort in a God who seemed to have forsaken them – I realized how unshakeable their faith was. It was more than just making wishes and having them come true, like Major Nelson did with Jeannie on TV. Even though their wishes weren't being granted, they still believed.

I helped my mom set the table and then I decided to go sit in the tree house until dinner. I half expected to find Lizzie and Scottie up there, but they weren't, so I was all alone.

27

I decided, as we were washing and drying the dinner dishes, that what I really needed was a good dose of the *Hardy Boys*. I was suspicious of two people: Mr. Anderson and Uncle Roy, and I didn't know where to go from there. I thought to myself, 'What would Frank and Joe do?' So, after we put the last dish in the cupboard, I told Lizzie that I felt like reading, but I didn't tell her why. We went to our bedroom, climbed up onto the top bunk, and opened our books. Even though it was summer, it was damp and a bit chilly, so we snuggled into our blankets.

I decided to re-read the very first *Hardy Boys* book, *The Tower Treasure*. I noticed that one of the first things that the boys did in the mystery was to write down the clues. That's what I needed to do, write down my clues about both Mr. Anderson and Uncle Roy. I pulled my notebook out from under my mattress.

Mr. Anderson:

    1. Photographs of naked girls in hidden office

    2. Was near Highland Terrace Dr. when Angela disappeared

Uncle Roy:

    1. Wears a uniform

    2. Had seen Angela earlier in the week

    3. Could easily have been near Highland Terrace Dr. when Angela disappeared

    4. Acted weird and sneaky in the squad car

That was it. Those were all the clues I had. Of course, thanks to us, Uncle Roy had tire tread molds from the road, the purple ribbon (and any fingerprints on it), and also the photograph of the naked girl at the Haunted Mansion. I was pretty sure that he could make Mr. Anderson look very guilty, and this would have made me happy, except that he had acted so strangely when I last talked with him. Uncle Roy was obviously hiding something. Instead of being excited when I gave him the evidence in the car, he had been distracted and disturbed. Was he guilty of something? If he was, then I was guilty, too, because I had aided and abetted the enemy. Because of me, Uncle Roy had all our evidence, and now he could either throw it away – or worse – he could use it to frame Mr. Anderson.

I couldn't take it anymore. I had to go try and find out if Uncle Roy had gone to question Mr. Anderson. After all, he had left our house with all of his men right after he talked to me. What could that mean? In my mind, it either meant that he felt like I was on to him, or it meant that he felt like he had enough evidence to question Mr. Anderson.

Since I couldn't ride my bike all the way downtown to police headquarters, I decided to go over to the Anderson's house to see if anything unusual was happening there. Even though it was late, it was still light outside, and I decided to pretend that I wanted to play with Nicky. I didn't tell Lizzie about my plans – I just got up and told her I'd be back in a second. And then, once I got outside, I sneaked across the street to Nicky's house.

❧ 28 ❧

I knocked on the kitchen door because that's the door I always went to when I wanted to play. I expected Nicky to answer the door, but no one came. I knocked one more time, just in case he was watching TV or something and couldn't hear me. Still, no one came. I decided to go look in the back yard. Sometimes, when Mrs. Anderson would do the laundry, she would keep the basement door open and Nicky would play in the yard. I opened the latch and looked around. I didn't see Nicky or even Baxter, which was strange. Usually, Baxter would be outside if everyone was gone. I walked over to the basement door; the same door that I had used to sneak into the house the night before. I tried the doorknob; it was unlocked.

I decided to go inside. I wasn't sure exactly what I was going to do once I got in there, but I just couldn't go back home and sit around and wait anymore. Maybe I'd try to get one more photo from the wall as evidence. I tiptoed through the laundry area and felt my way towards the back hall – I didn't need the light anymore – I knew exactly where I was going. The special bookcase-door was closed and I walked up to it and stood perfectly still. I was listening for sounds of movement to make sure that Mr. Anderson wasn't in his secret room, but I couldn't hear anything. I walked back to the laundry area and squinted my eyes as I looked around the dark basement. Where in the world was Baxter? Was I too late? Had the police already come and thrown the entire family in jail, even the dog? I needed to get into the secret room, so I reached under the shelf, inside the bookcase and found the knothole. It was easy this time, but my hand was shaking so much that I had to steady it with the other hand in order to push the button. It clicked open and I instantly heard barking and movement. Baxter was stuck in the secret room! I pushed the door open.

"Bax," I whispered, "what're you doing in here?"

"The question is, what are *you* doing in here, Young Lady?" an angry voice said from the other side of the door. I screamed and fell on my bottom. Baxter thought that I was playing with him, so he climbed on top of me and started to lick my face.

"Baxter, heel!" Mr. Anderson said sternly. I just sat there, looking up at him, wanting with all of my heart to turn around and flee, but thinking that I might have a better chance by talking my way out.

"I'm sorry to disturb you. I was – uh – just looking for Nicky. Is he home?" I was slowly crab-walking backwards out of the hall, hoping that Mr. Anderson wouldn't notice. But he walked toward me until he was standing over me, one leg on either side of my body.

"So, you were looking for Nicky, were you?" he said, and little flecks of spit flew out of his mouth and landed on me.

"Yes, Sir. Sorry to bother you," I said. "I'll just be going." I turned on my hands and knees and started to crawl quickly toward the laundry area, but Mr. Anderson grabbed my waist with both of his hands and lifted me up. I started to wriggle and kick, but he pulled me tightly against his body and then backed up into the secret room. Baxter was jumping up on us excitedly, and Mr. Anderson lifted his left foot and kicked him right in the gut. He then used the same foot to kick the door shut. I could hear poor Baxter crying on the other side of the door. I was squirming in Mr. Anderson's arms, trying to get loose, but he wrapped one arm around both of my arms, and held me against his chest. I was unable to budge. I purposely relaxed so that he would loosen his hold, but instead, he walked over to his desk with me still gripped football-style in one arm. He grabbed a metal letter opener and held the sharp point up to my face.

"See this, Sweetheart?" he said. He slid the point lightly down my cheek. "This is what I will use on you over and over again if you even try to move, or if you make a sound. Am I making myself clear?"

I nodded my head. I didn't utter a sound, but my thoughts were going crazy. Was he acting this way because he was guilty of kidnapping Angela? Or was he just mad because he had caught me snooping? I didn't think that a normal dad would threaten to stab a kid for snooping, but I still had it in the back of my mind that Uncle Roy might be the guilty one. Mr. Anderson finally put me down in a chair.

"Okay, this is what we're going to do," he said. "I'm going to let you sit right here for a minute while I go get some rope, do you hear me?" I nodded my head. "Okay, if you're a good little girl, you won't get hurt." He backed his way toward the door. I didn't know how to open the door from the inside once it had clicked shut, so I watched him carefully. I was already planning my escape. The door was made of a rough wood. It wasn't sanded or painted and it was really grainy looking. Mr. Anderson pressed his finger in an area on the right edge of the door and there was another clicking noise. The door popped in ever so slightly and he was able to grab the end of the door and pull it towards him. He was gone for just a second and then he came back with a rope in his hands. Baxter had come in with him this time, but he scurried under the desk. Mr. Anderson quickly tied my legs and arms to the chair.

I was trying to look relaxed, but was secretly using an old *Hardy Boys* trick. I flexed my muscles as he was tying me up so that when he was done – and when he was gone – I could relax my body which, according to every *Hardy Boys* book that I had ever read, would leave a bit of slack in the rope. I hoped that there would be enough slack that I could loosen the rope around my wrist and wriggle my way out. I also hoped that Mr. Anderson would leave after he finished tying me. But he sat in the other chair and crossed his legs. He put one elbow on his knee and then rested his chin in his hand. He looked at me with his eyes half closed and a strange smile on his face.

"So you were looking for little Nicky, huh?" he asked me, and the look he gave me made a shudder run through my body. He did not look like the nice Mr. Anderson who had played with us in the back yard. I didn't say anything. I just nodded my head. He stood up and walked to the door.

"You won't be playing with Nicky anymore, you little sneak," he hissed. He turned and left the room, slamming the secret door shut, leaving Baxter and me in the room.

I was weak with relief. Once he was gone, Baxter came out from under the desk and walked over to me. He whimpered and nudged my leg with his wet nose and then he licked my face. Sweet puppy. He wanted to comfort me. We were comrades now. I wanted to feel sorry for myself, but I knew that I did not have time for self-pity. Instead, I checked to see if the ropes were loose. Amazingly, they were – but not loose enough to slip out of. I began to wriggle my wrists to try to loosen them some more. I used my thumbs on the knots, but it was a lot harder than I thought it would be. I could hear Mr. Anderson walking around upstairs, which was making me feel panicky. I began to take deep breaths. Every few minutes, I had to take a break, because I was getting tired.

I remembered the first time I discovered the secret room and how I thought that it would be cool if there was a secret tunnel that led from this room, under the street, into my house. Now, I found myself thinking about that idea again. If only I could get the stupid ropes off, then I would move the desk to uncover the hidden door that led to the tunnel. I would crawl through the tunnel and end up in my basement, in the corner under the front of the house, where we kept all our bicycles. If only, I thought.

Before Angela went missing, my dad had been talking about taking us to a bicycling event in July in a small town outside of Seattle, but still within King County. He said that it was the size of Richland and was called Redmond, and it would almost be like taking a trip back home again. The main event was a twenty-five mile bicycle race around Lake Sammamish, but there would be a parade, too, and lots of food. The food would probably be fish, because my dad told us that there was so much salmon nearby that the town used to be named Salmonberg. I knew we wouldn't be able to buy any food there, but for once, I was glad. I preferred my mom's peanut butter and jelly sandwiches to fish any day. I wasn't sure how Daddy planned to get all of us kids and our bicycles in the station wagon, but I couldn't wait for the Redmond Derby Days…

My body jerked and I opened my eyes to see Mr. Anderson standing in front of me. I must have fallen asleep. I hadn't heard him come back. Normally, Baxter would have been barking excitedly at the return of his owner, but he was hiding under the desk, afraid of the man he no longer knew. I felt the same way.

Mr. Anderson walked over to one of the pictures that was pinned to the wall, and stared at it. He then looked at another picture and then another as he circled around the room. He was mumbling to himself and touching the images of the naked girls on the wall next to me. I looked at his face. I felt certain at that moment that Mr. Anderson was the one. He was the man who had taken Angela. He took his eyes off of the pictures and focused his gaze back on me.

"You know, Little Bobbi," Mr. Anderson said, as he walked over to me, "I have been watching you for a long time now. You are quite something to look at – quite something." He put his hand on my cheek and then he ran his fingers through my hair. I clenched my jaw. I was beginning to feel nauseous.

"You would be a nice addition to my collection, don't you think?" he said, and he waved his hand at the walls that surrounded us. He then leaned down and pressed his mouth against my ear. "Yes," he whispered, "I think you would make a very nice addition indeed." He moved his face so that he was staring directly into my eyes. "I like the young ones," he said. "I especially like the young ones." He leaned towards me to kiss my mouth. I was revolted, and I tried to turn my head away. His wet lips caught the corner of my mouth and I gagged. He pulled his face away and I gagged again. Mr. Anderson quickly backed away from me with a disgusted look on his face. He moved to the other side of the room and then turned around toward me again. He made a growling noise deep in his throat.

"You had better be careful, Little Girl," he said menacingly. "You don't want to make Mr. Anderson angry." He looked around the room. "Just ask any of these girls," he continued. "They will tell you that it is not advisable to make me mad." I glanced up at him. His eyes looked like they were going to pop out of their sockets. I wasn't sure if he was completely out of his mind or if he was just trying to scare me, but the way he looked suddenly struck me as being funny and a giggle slipped out before I could control it. He took a step toward me and slapped my face. I closed my eyes as the tears started to trickle down my cheeks. I couldn't wipe them off, and I couldn't keep them from coming. I gulped some air and tried to calm down. I felt like if I let myself fall apart, he might hit me again. I didn't dare look at him again, but I decided that I had to ask him some questions right then. I felt like I might not have another chance to do it.

"Mr. Anderson," I said, "I was wondering where you keep your uniform?"

His eyes got wide for a moment, and then he smiled. "How'd you know I wore a uniform?" he asked. He turned and walked over to a shelf in the corner of the room, where there were magazines and camera equipment and some clothes. He picked up an olive green shirt that looked like it had just been ironed, and a pair of crisp, green pants. Pinned to the shirt was a badge of some kind. He draped the outfit over his chair.

"Nice, isn't it?" he asked. "Know where I got it?" I shook my head. "At the army surplus store – the boys coming back from Vietnam can't give them away fast enough," he said. "I got this for almost nothing." I thought of all the war protests that I had seen on TV, and I knew that he wasn't exaggerating. He grinned at me and then carefully folded the shirt and pants and put them back on the shelf. He reached for the camera.

"Mr. Anderson!" I yelled, "I will never, *ever* let you take a picture of me! I just want to know where my sister is! Do you hear me? I need to know – what did you do with my sister?"

Mr. Anderson smiled at me and then he started to laugh. His body began to shake and he doubled over, holding his sides. I didn't know why he was laughing and I didn't want to know. But I wanted him to stop and he wouldn't. He just wouldn't.

I sat there, tied up in my chair and I began to cry because I knew – beyond a shadow of a doubt – that he had done something despicable to my sister, Angela.

❧ 30 ❧

He noticed that I was crying and he told me to stop. By that time, I was slightly hysterical, and I couldn't stop crying. He came over to me and slapped me across the face again.

"Shut up!" he screamed, and then he bent over and looked directly into my eyes. "Did you hear me?" he shouted. "I told you to shut up!" And then he hit me again. My head jerked to the side, but I could see him as he walked away. He was nursing his right hand. My body was convulsing as I tried with all of my might to stop crying. I could taste blood inside my mouth, but I knew if I didn't stop crying he would come back. I was thinking of Angela. How long had she been in the clutches of this crazy person? I had very little hope in my heart that we would ever find her alive. I decided that I really did not have anything to lose at that point so, once I was able to breathe normally again, I asked Mr. Anderson to take me to my sister. He kind of sneered at me and made a fist like he was going to hit me if I didn't stop talking, but I didn't care.

"Take me to my sister. I want to be with my sister, please!" I just kept saying those words over and over and over and finally, instead of hitting me, instead of untying me and putting me in the car to grant me my request, he got up and took a bandana that was in his pocket and tied it around my mouth. He then grabbed a roll of thick tape and wrapped it around the bandana. I was afraid he was going to tape over my nose and suffocate me, but he wrapped the tape around my mouth and around the back of my head a couple of times, and then he put the roll of tape down and left. He shut the door behind him, leaving Baxter in the room.

Baxter was a comfort to me. He sat right at my feet, loyal and patient as can be. I was still trying to get loose from the ropes, but by now my wrists were bleeding and my muscles ached from the strain. I was praying with all my might that Lizzie would start to miss me, and that she would go to my parents. But I realized that it was very possible that Lizzie had fallen asleep reading her book and that my parents had never checked on us that evening. They knew we were reading – why should they check on us? That left Scottie; surely, he would have seen that I wasn't in my bed, but then my discouraged heart told me that it was possible that he had seen Lizzie and thought that the two of us had fallen asleep on the top bunk. It had happened before.

And so, I was being very realistic when I thought to myself that I was doomed. Or, maybe not doomed, but definitely stuck in that room, tied up to that chair, for at least as long as it took either Lizzie or Scottie to think of looking there for me. I just hoped that Mr. Anderson would not be the one to come back first. I knew that he had left the house. I'd heard the door slam earlier and his car engine start, but I wasn't sure if he was leaving for good or if he had plans to return to torture me further. I felt confused. I did not want him to come back – I thought that I would die if he ever touched me again, but I also did not want him to get away.

I tried to scream, but all that came out was a kind of muffled cry. It was pitiful – so much for being a hero.

Before they had ever thought of looking for me, the police found the place where Angela had been hidden. It was raining and dark, and even though it was late June, it was cold. It turned out that Uncle Roy had taken all of our clues down to police headquarters, and he had convinced his chief that he possessed enough evidence on Mr. Anderson to pull him in for questioning.

It had been easy for the police to prove that Mr. Anderson's tire treads matched the tire tread molds that they had taken on the shoulder of Highland Terrace Drive. Apparently, that is what Uncle Roy had assigned the policemen who had been staying in our kitchen to do that evening during our dinner. Those policemen had sneaked over to our neighbor's house and had carefully taken pictures of his tires. They'd taken the film downtown and had it developed, and once they'd compared the pictures to the molds from the side of the road and discovered that they matched, they brought Mr. Anderson in for questioning. Mr. Anderson was just returning to his home where Baxter and I were locked up when the policemen pulled into his yard and picked him up. I never heard a thing.

As it turned out, Mr. Anderson was a weak, cowardly man. The minute they had him in police custody and started to pepper him with questions, he blurted out his terrible confession. All he asked – all he wanted – was for the police to promise him that they wouldn't tell his wife. The police said that they couldn't guarantee anything, but that he should just give himself up because they already knew everything.

"It's all over, Man. We know about the girls in the woods and in that old house, we know about the pictures you took, and we know about the Johnson girl. And that's what we want to talk about right now. Tell us where the Johnson girl is."

Mr. Anderson's mouth fell open. He realized that somehow the cops had caught him, and he began to sob uncontrollably as he poured out his story. Mr. Anderson had gotten into the habit of pulling his car onto the shoulder of Highland Terrace Drive once a week around the time that the high school let out. It was that stretch of road where there were no houses. He would wait in the woods when the kids would make their way home using the shortcut. He found that if he started to talk to some of the girls, they would let him walk with them; and once he had spent a bit of time talking with a girl, he explained, it was much easier to gain her trust.

He would ultimately steer a girl toward the abandoned house. Once he got her there, he would offer her pot, and after the girl got high, he would tell her his secret. The story he gave was that he was in Seattle scouting for new talent for Hollywood. He was looking for girls who would fit the bill – did she know of anyone?

"Of course," he said with a cocky laugh, "the girl would always suggest herself." He closed his eyes, re-living his memories. "Every girl wants to be a star. Then, all I needed was a camera – it was that easy." He waved his hand in the air. "Just hold a camera," he explained, "and girls will take off their clothes." He began to laugh as he leaned back in the chair and put his feet up on the desk. The police officer stood up and knocked his feet off of the desk with a grunt. Mr. Anderson didn't even seem to notice. He was caught up in his story and he had a captive audience.

He hadn't been planning anything on June third, but, after leaving his house that day, he was driving back to work by way of Highland Terrace Drive, and he saw a pretty teenage girl walking on the side of the road. He was running late, but he couldn't help himself. He pulled the car over, got out of it, and offered the girl a ride. He didn't realize that he was talking to Angela, the girl from across the street. He started to tell her how pretty she was, and that he would like to get to know her. He closed his eyes, getting lost in his memories. The cop nearest him quickly brought him back by shaking him on the shoulder. Mr. Anderson glared at the policeman, but he carried on with his story. By the time Angela told him who she was, he had already said too much. He admitted to the police that he should have left her standing on the side of the road, and driven away. But he was afraid that Angela would tell his wife about him. He couldn't take that chance, so he grabbed her by the arm and shoved her into the car. The police determined that Angela's ribbon must have fallen out of her hair at that point – she had not gotten into his car willingly.

Mr. Anderson explained to the police that he panicked and drove around town for a while with Angela in his car. It wasn't until he had circled back into his own neighborhood again that he remembered the abandoned house. He decided to take Angela there, at least until he could come up with a plan. Once they got to the house, he dragged her into the basement. There were photographs that he had taken pinned up all over the walls. He warned her that if she made a sound, or tried to get away, he would take pictures of her and show them to her parents. That was how he convinced Angela to cooperate with him.

There were still tools and scattered debris in the garage of the basement, and Mr. Anderson found a rope and some rags and tied Angela up and gagged her. He was going to leave her there, but it was damp and chilly, so he decided to start a fire on the concrete floor to keep her warm overnight. Something went wrong, and before he knew it, the whole basement was on fire. Mr. Anderson tried to put the fire out, but the house was full of trash and dried wood, and the fire got out of control before he could do anything about it. He grabbed Angela, threw her over his shoulder, and ran to his car and stuffed her into his trunk. He then screeched away before anyone in the neighborhood noticed the fire. The cops later found his tire tracks deeply etched into the mud in the front yard of the old burned-down house.

Mr. Anderson instinctively drove toward his office downtown. Once he got there, he had to decide what to do with Angela. His job was near an underground tourist spot called Pioneer Square, which was an actual city street that was destroyed by the Great Seattle Fire in June of 1889. After the fire, the city built a new Pioneer Square on top of the old. Years later, the original Pioneer Square was partially restored and opened to the public. On lunch hours, Mr. Anderson would sometimes take the underground tour, but he would break off from the group and hide himself in one of the storefronts, so that he could secretly watch people.

That evening, Mr. Anderson had waited until after dark, and then pulled into the empty parking lot on First Avenue. He had untied Angela's legs because there were six flights of stairs to walk down to get to the main street. He took Angela deep into Pioneer Square, to a secluded area in the very back of one of the buildings. And that is where he kept her for all those weeks.

Upon hearing the confession, the police immediately rushed to Pioneer Square and went deep into the bowels of nineteenth century downtown Seattle in search of Angela. They found the remains of a campfire and a glass milk bottle that had a little water in it, but Angela was not there. They were too late.

The police called our parents and told them that they had Mr. Anderson in their custody. They explained that he had confessed that he was the one who had taken Angela – my parents were shocked and overwhelmed. They couldn't believe that their own neighbor had anything to do with the tragic disappearance of their oldest daughter. They had all but given up on the idea of ever seeing Angela alive again, but now they had renewed hope. They awakened the family with the incredible news and told everyone to get into the car. When I didn't show up, my mother was irritated.

"Where could she have gone to so early?" she said to no one in particular. She wrote a note for me and left it on the kitchen counter, and then the six of them got into the car to go down to police headquarters.

Once they arrived, my mom and dad, Graham, Adele, Scottie and Lizzie all rushed into the station. The police were in the process of questioning Mr. Anderson in a back room, so my parents were not allowed to see him, but my dad went right up to the counter and told the officer behind it that he needed to talk to his neighbor immediately. The policeman promptly asked my dad and the rest of the family to take a seat – someone would come and talk with them soon. Mom was very anxious. She couldn't force herself to sit down, so she paced back and forth.

"I just wonder what Bobbi was up to this morning," she said. "I sure hope that she saw my note." And then she continued pacing.

I had fallen into an uncomfortable sleep, waking up every hour or so with a jolt. I was still trying to twist and pull the ropes off, but my wrists were raw and my arms kept falling asleep. I was so glad to have Baxter there for company. He stayed at my feet for most of the time, but every once in a while, he would walk around the small room, stopping to scratch at the closed door. And then he would return to my side, usually licking my knee once before settling back down next to me. I knew he had to be thirsty, poor thing. I was thirsty too.

As I was sitting there, desperately trying to think of a way for the two of us to escape, I realized that the same song had been running over and over in my head. It was from an album by Simon and Garfunkel that Graham and Angela had secretly purchased. They would play the record when our parents weren't around. The lyrics were soothing, like a prayer:

When you're weary, feeling small.

When tears are in your eyes, I will dry them all.

I'm on your side.

When times get rough, and friends just can't be found,

Like a bridge over troubled water,

I will lay me down.

Like a bridge over troubled water,

I will lay me down.

I had no idea where Lizzie and Scottie were and why they hadn't come to rescue me. I would have thought that once I didn't come back home, somebody would have noticed, and that they would have tried to figure out where I was. Hadn't anyone missed me? Even though I knew that a real sleuth was supposed to be brave (I could never remember even one time when Frank or Joe had broken down) I became more and more despondent as the night wore on. I wanted my mommy.

As I sat there in that dark room, tied up and immobile, waiting to be discovered, I remembered another time when I was desperate to be found by my parents. My family had taken a vacation out East. We had been visiting Liberty Island, the land mass that held the famous Statue of Liberty. It was extremely exciting to be so close to the national monument. We couldn't wait to get up into the crown and to look out over the harbor. The lines to get into the statue were really long, so Scottie and I decided to take a different line from the rest of the family. We thought that our line would be faster.

"We'll meet you when we get back down," we said to our family, and off we ran. I am sure that our parents called out to us, but we hadn't stopped to listen. It never occurred to Scottie and me that we might get in to trouble. We always lived for the moment and, up until that point, we had never run into any serious problems. On that particular summer day in New York City, Scottie and I found that our line had, indeed, been faster than the line that the rest of our family had stood in, but, in the end, we got completely separated from them. We scrambled around and looked everywhere, but we could not find them. One ferry after the next left the island, and each time one left, we were afraid that our family members were leaving with it. After awhile, Scottie and I began to panic. We got to the point where we felt certain that our parents must have thought that we had gone on ahead and – in their desperation to find us – had taken a ferry back to Manhattan, inadvertently leaving us on Liberty Island.

We finally decided that the only thing to do was to try to catch up with them, so we headed for the ferry line ourselves. We were just about to get on the next boat when we heard our father call our names. Both Scottie and I ran with all our might and threw ourselves into our daddy's arms. I remember the feeling of total relief that washed over my body as he hugged me.

Our parents were not very happy with us. Who knows how many hours Scottie and I had been separated from the rest of the family? We had definitely worried our parents half to death, and probably our siblings, too. But luckily for Scottie and me, as angry as our parents were at us, they were ultimately very happy to have us back in their arms.

And that's what I was thinking of; being back in my parents' arms. I had to believe that they were searching for me high and low – just like they had on Liberty Island – that they hadn't yet thought to search across the street from their own house, but that they would very soon…

33

Down at the police station my mom hung up the phone for the sixth time.

"She's not home yet," she told my father. "Where in the world could she have gone?"

"I'm sure she's fine, Mother," my father said. "She probably came back from riding her bike or picking strawberries or whatever took her fancy this morning, saw your note, and decided to go out front and wait for us in that tree she loves so much. She wouldn't be able to hear the phone out there," he pointed out to her.

The kids, except for Lizzie and Scottie, were all huddled around a small black and white TV that was playing in the corner of the lobby. Scottie and Lizzie had been standing by my parents, waiting to hear of my whereabouts. After my dad's explanation, they nodded to each other, relieved. Of course, I would be waiting in 'The Best Climbing Tree in Washington'. They left my parents and joined the other kids in front of the television set.

"Mr. Johnson?" A police officer said as he came out of a back room. My father nodded and walked over to him. "We have reason to believe that your neighbor, Mr. Anderson has seen your daughter today."

"Today?" my father asked. "Then she is alive?" He reached out and grabbed the arm of the police officer.

"Well, Sir," the officer replied, "we can't be positive of that. But you have our permission to go and speak with him."

"Take me to him," my father said immediately. He then turned to my mother and kissed her cheek. "I have a good feeling about this, Sweetheart. I think we are going to get Angela back today."

"Oh, Daddy, I hope you're right," my mom whispered to him as he turned to go. The two men walked down the dark hall. One of the fluorescent lights in the ceiling was flickering and the other was burnt out completely. When they reached the end of the hall, the policeman knocked on a door and then opened it.

"I have Mr. Johnson here, Sir," he told the officer in charge.

"Send him in," the officer replied. Inside the room, there was a long table. A detective sat on one side the table, and Mr. Anderson sat directly opposite him. My father walked right up to Mr. Anderson, trying to hold back his anger.

"Mike, where have you put my daughter?" my father asked the man, but he just looked at him through swollen, blood-shot eyes. After a moment, he spoke.

"Which one?" he asked my father, and then he laughed as if he had just told a joke. My father looked at the detective questioningly.

"Is he delusional?" he asked him.

"No. He has been completely lucid for the past hour," the officer replied. Then he looked at Mr. Anderson.

"No funny business, Buddy. Just answer your neighbor's question. Where is the girl?" Mr. Anderson looked at the detective and then at my father.

"Never mind me, just never mind," he said. "The brunette is in the trunk," he said, "but you'd better hurry."

"In the trunk?" my father exploded. "Are you telling me that my daughter is in the trunk of your car?" He turned to the detective. "Could this be true?" he asked. "Where is his car? Do we know where it is?" My father could hardly contain his impatience.

"His car is in the driveway of his home," the detective said as he stood up and grabbed the radio that was on his belt. "We picked him up in front of his house as he was getting out of his car." He spoke into the radio and, after some back and forth, told my father that there was an officer in the area, and that he was heading over to our neighborhood immediately. My father crossed over to Mr. Anderson. He reached down and grabbed the front of his shirt with both hands.

"Is she alive?" he asked him hoarsely, as he lifted the man out of his seat.

"Mr. Johnson, that will be enough!" the detective said as he snapped his fingers. The nearest officer immediately rushed over to my father and pulled him away from Mr. Anderson.

"You ask him, then," my father said. He stood nose to nose with the detective. "Ask him if my daughter is alive!" he demanded. He took two steps back from my father and then looked at Mr. Anderson.

"You'd better pray that that girl is alive, Anderson," the detective warned him.

Mr. Anderson folded his arms in front of his chest and said, "I'm not talking." And then he began to laugh again. As the policemen took Mr. Anderson away, they told my father that he was free to go back home.

"Meet us at your neighbor's house," they instructed. My father returned to my mother and the rest of the family and told them to come with him. He urged them to hurry; they were going to meet the policemen at our home. Scottie dragged his feet a bit. There was only a minute left to the show that they had been watching, but Lizzie grabbed him.

"Scottie," she said, "hurry up. They may have found your sister." Lizzie's words seemed to awaken him, and he quickly ran after the rest of the family.

34

I was in agony. My legs and my arms were cramped and my wrists were throbbing with pain. I realized by lunchtime that I was not going to be able to wriggle out of the ropes. I was worried about Baxter – he hadn't gotten up and walked around for a long time.

I vaguely remember hearing sirens and hoping that someone was coming to rescue me. But then I think I dozed off again. It was Baxter who brought me out of my fog. He was barking and scratching at the door with all his strength. I was confused at first. Was it just that Baxter needed to go out and was feeling desperate? Or was it possible that someone was actually here to look for us? Why had he suddenly become so agitated? And then I heard something. There were people outside. I could hear them talking. I couldn't tell what they were saying, but they were there, and I wanted to yell out to them, 'I'm here. Please, save me!' But the only noise I could make sounded more like a cat meowing than a human being pleading for her life. Thankfully, Baxter was making up for my silence. He was barking wildly. I was sure that someone would hear him. I just knew that someone would take pity on a frantic dog.

❧ ❧

My father pulled the station wagon into our driveway. On the way home, he had filled my mother in on his conversation with Mr. Anderson. Once he turned off the car, they both jumped out and ran across the street to join the policemen who were already working on getting the trunk door open on Mr. Anderson's car. They didn't have the key, so they were using a pry bar to pop the trunk. What they found when they finally got it open was the tiny body of a girl curled up in the fetal position.

"Angela!" my parents screamed, but she did not respond. My father reached into the car and scooped her into his arms. He pressed her to his chest while my mother held her wrist and felt for a heartbeat.

"Is she alive?" my father asked, his voice cracking.

"Oh, Daddy," she cried, "I think I feel a pulse!" At just about that time the ambulance wailed and careened its way down the road and into the front yard that belonged to Mr. Anderson. The paramedics jumped out of the ambulance and quickly told my father to put Angela onto the stretcher. My whole family stepped back as they began treating my sister. They put the stretcher in the ambulance and asked who would like to accompany her. My mother hopped into the back of vehicle before they even finished their question. Daddy, my brothers and sister, and Lizzie waved to the ambulance as it sped away. Once the sirens faded into the distance, Lizzie looked at Scottie.

"Where's Bobbi?" she asked. My father overheard Lizzie.

"Yes, where *is* Bobbi?" he repeated. "Let's go find her." And they headed over to our house.

⌒ ⌒

I could hear the ambulance. I could hear the people talking excitedly, and then, I could hear the silence. The silence was the loudest. Baxter was frantic. He, too, could hear the action above us and he seemed to understand that it was now or never. He howled like a wolf to the moon, but no one heard him. After a while, he came back to me and looked into my eyes. He seemed to be asking for forgiveness, as if he had let me down somehow. I wanted to tell him that it wasn't his fault. He had tried his best and I loved him for it. My mind was spinning in a million different directions. Why had there been sirens? Had they caught Mr. Anderson? Would they be able to get him to tell them where he had hidden me and – more importantly – where he had hidden Angela? I could only hope and pray.

⌒ ⌒

My dad thought that maybe I might have left a note where my mom's note had been. But when they got back to the house, Mon's note was still sitting on the counter where she'd left it. My dad slid behind the table and sat down.

"Where could she be?" he said out loud to both Lizzie and Scottie. "When was the last time any of us actually saw her?" He looked first at Scottie and then at Lizzie. Lizzie spoke up nervously.

"I probably should have mentioned this earlier," she said, "but with all the excitement, I didn't think about it. Last night, Bobbi and I were reading on her top bunk. I kept kinda falling asleep while I read. I remember that Bobbi told me she'd be right back at some point during the evening, and I figured she was just going to

149

the bathroom or something. The next thing I knew I was waking up this morning when you were calling us."

"Did Bobbi ever come back to your room?" my dad asked her.

"I thought that she had," Lizzie replied. "She wasn't in bed when I woke up, but you know Bobbi – she always wakes up earlier than I do. It didn't seem all that strange that she wasn't in the room when I woke up. But now I'm worried, Mr. Johnson," she said. "I don't know where she could possibly be."

Lizzie looked at my father with a pitiful look on her face. "I'm so sorry. I probably should have told you that I was feeling worried earlier, you know, when we were down at the police station." Lizzie twirled her hair around her finger. "I just don't remember if she ever came back to bed…"

"Lizzie, don't you feel bad for one minute," my father said comfortingly. "You're right – we all thought that Bobbi had just gone off on one of her adventures. Now, why don't the two of you sit down," he said as he pointed to the bench seat. Lizzie and Scottie both sat down and looked at my father expectantly. "Let's take a few minutes and think. Where do we suppose Bobbi could have gone? What was on her mind? What kind of plans had you all made for today? Had Bobbi been talking with Jimmy yesterday? Could she have gone and met him without asking us?"

Lizzie spoke up quickly. "Oh, no, Mr. Johnson," she said emphatically. "Bobbi was not doing anything sneaky! If anything, she has been so worried about Angela that she's been ignoring her friends lately. We went to our room last night to read because we were both tired. The only thing that I noticed that was kind of weird was that, while we were reading, Bobbi kept writing something in her notebook." Lizzie jumped off the bench. "I'll be right back," she said and she dashed out of the kitchen. She returned in a few minutes with the notebook and handed it over to my dad.

"This is it," Lizzie said. "She was acting like she didn't want me to notice that she was writing in it, so I didn't ask her what she was doing." Just then the telephone rang. My dad jumped up and answered it. The kids could hear my mom crying through the receiver.

"Honey, slow down. I can't understand what you are saying," my dad said calmly. "Uh-huh, uh-huh. That's what the doctor said? Really? And what does that mean? Uh-huh. Really? So, when can we all come down? Wonderful. That's just wonderful. God is good. What's that? No, not yet, but don't you worry. We'll find her. Okay, then, Darling. Thanks for calling. I love you, too."

Graham and Adele flew into the kitchen; they had been in their bedrooms, just waiting for my mother's call. My dad turned around after hanging up the phone. Tears were streaming down his cheeks, but he had a smile on his face.

"She is going to be okay!" he told the kids exuberantly. "She is weak and dehydrated, and she has lost a lot of weight, but the doctors say that in about a week, she should be strong enough to come home." Everybody started to cry and hug each other. Scottie got up on his chair and did little jig.

"Hooray, we found Angela!" he shouted. My dad swooped him into his arms and gave him a squeeze.

"Let's not break our neck while your mother is gone, okay?" he said as he placed him back on the floor. Daddy looked around at his little family with a big smile on his face. "Okay then, Kids, let's find Bobbi now and everything will be right in the world."

For the first time in a long time he felt like he could relax. There was just this little problem of figuring out where his fourth child had run off to.

35

My father picked up the notebook again. "All right, let's take a look at what you've got here, Lizzie," he said.

Graham and Adele joined Lizzie and Scottie at the table. My dad glanced through the pages from the beginning and then he turned to the last entry. "It looks like she has made notes here about Mr. Anderson and your uncle, Lizzie. What do you think that was about?"

Scottie spoke up first. "Well you know, Dad, that Bobbi has been spending all her time trying to find Angela. The three of us have been gathering evidence for a month, right Lizzie?" He looked at Lizzie and she nodded. "Yesterday," he continued, "Bobbi met Uncle Roy and gave him all the evidence."

Lizzie nodded her head again. "Yes, it was yesterday morning," Lizzie said, "but she came back from meeting with him acting all weird. I couldn't get her to tell me what my uncle and she had talked about."

"What does the notebook say, Dad?" Scottie asked, getting excited. My dad placed the notebook on the table so that every one of the kids could look at the words:

Mr. Anderson:

1. Photographs of naked girls in hidden office
2. Was near Highland Terrace Dr. when Angela disappeared

Uncle Roy:

1. Wears a uniform
2. Had seen Angela earlier in the week
3. Could easily have been near Highland Terrace Dr. when Angela disappeared
4. Acted weird and sneaky in the squad car

"Oh my goodness," my dad exclaimed. "It looks like Bobbi had begun to suspect your uncle, Lizzie!"

"She *what?*" Lizzie turned the paper so that she could see it better. She then slowly sat back down in her chair. "Oh," she exclaimed, "so that's what she was talking about."

"What, Honey? What had Bobbi been talking about?" my father asked her. He was such a gentle man, but he couldn't hide his anxiety. Lizzie started to twist her hair around her finger again.

"Bobbi came back from talking with my uncle and she was saying things like 'Can we trust policemen?' She was talking about the fact that policemen wear uniforms – I don't know." Lizzie's eyes filled with tears. "I guess she must have been thinking that Uncle Roy had taken Angela because he wore a uniform. I should have been paying better attention. I'm sorry."

"It's okay, Lizzie," my father said. "Here's the question, and I think that you and Scottie would know the answer to this better than anybody. How would Bobbi have tried to solve this mystery at this point? Where do you think she went?"

"That's easy," Scottie said, "she would have gone and talked with Uncle Roy again. You know, gotten him to answer all her questions."

"Yeah, but Uncle Roy and all the other policeman had already left, remember?" Lizzie reminded Scottie. "So, the only way to talk with him would have been to go all the way downtown." Lizzie then looked at my father. "Bobbi would never have done that without telling us," she said. "She knows how worried everyone has been about Angela being missing"

"But she would have done something, right?" my dad asked.

Lizzie suddenly stood up. "I know where she is! I know where she is!" she exclaimed, and ran out of the kitchen.

"Where is she going?" Adele asked excitedly.

"I'm not sure. But why don't you and Graham stay here in case your mother calls again," my dad said, as he ran toward the door. He hesitated for a moment. "Scottie," he yelled over his shoulder, "I think you need to come along." Scottie didn't need any more encouragement; he raced out the kitchen door after Lizzie and my dad.

Scottie found them standing on the sidewalk outside. "Lizzie, are you thinking what I'm thinking?" he asked her.

"Yes, Scottie," Lizzie replied. "She went to talk to Mr. Anderson. Where else would she have gone? And if he was there, and she accused him of taking your sister, you know that he would never let her get away."

"Do you think that she got caught by Mr. Anderson?" Scottie asked Lizzie, as my father began to pace next to them on the sidewalk.

"I don't know, but I do think that she went over to ask him a few questions," Lizzie said. "I think that she was tired of waiting around for the police to figure it out, and that she took matters into her own hands." Scottie nodded his head.

"Lizzie, I think you're right." He looked at our father. "Follow us, Dad," he said, and he grabbed Lizzie's hand and ran with her across the street to the Anderson's.

It was Baxter who first picked up on the activity that was going on outside. His head came up and then his body followed. He pranced right over to the door and began to scratch and bark.

"Is that you, Baxter?" Somebody yelled from the other side of the door. Was that Scottie? Yes, I was sure of it. It was Scottie. I felt weak with relief.

"Don't worry, Bobbi," Lizzie shouted, "We're going to get you out of there!" Scottie and Lizzie – I knew that they would come for me. I just knew it! I tried to acknowledge that I could hear them, but all that came out was a grunt. Baxter, on the other hand, had come to life. He was barking and jumping and scratching. I was praying with all that was in me that Lizzie would remember how to open the door. Had she been paying attention when I had pushed the button hidden in the knothole? I heard the telltale click, and then saw the door shift in. She had! Lizzie had found the button! Slowly the door was being pushed open into the room. The first face I saw was Lizzie's.

"Oh, Bobbi!" she screamed, "I'm so sorry!" I was smiling behind the tape and the bandana. I had never seen anything more wonderful than Lizzie's face and then Scottie's and then my dad's. Daddy raced across the room and held my face in his hands before he even started to try to untie the ropes. He looked deep into my eyes as if to see if I was okay and, at the same time, to communicate to me that I was going to be okay, that he was going to take good care of me. Tears rushed into my eyes.

Scottie found a pair of scissors on the workbench and brought it into to the secret room. They had me out of the ropes within a few minutes and – for the second time that day – my dad scooped one of his daughters into his arms and carried her to safety.

When I finally saw Angela in a cold green hospital room in downtown Seattle, I almost didn't recognize her. It was evil, what he had done to her, pure evil. I had always tried to close my eyes to it before – always tried to see good in people, but I couldn't pretend anymore: evil did exist. I realized right then that I could never afford to keep my eyes closed to it again.

My father had told us, when we were digging for clams on the beach, that geoducks had very few predators. That was the reason they were able to survive so long and get so big. And up until June, I thought that we were safe like that too, that we had no real enemies. I guess I grew up that summer. I learned the harsh lesson that there were predators out there, and that they were always looking to consume the very vulnerable, the very innocent.

Uncle Roy visited Angela and me when we were in the hospital. The doctors decided to keep me there overnight. Lizzie told Uncle Roy about me suspecting him after our conversation in his squad car, and I guess he felt really bad.

"Bobbi," he said to me, as I lay there on the hospital bed, "I am so sorry that I made you feel uncomfortable that morning when we talked. All the time that you were filling me in on the clues that you and your friends had found, I was thinking about how embarrassed I was that we professionals had so entirely missed the boat!" He made a sheepish face, and then stood up and started to pace. "I was really mortified, you know? I mean, there you were, you three kids, figuring out details in this case that the entire Seattle Police Department had missed." Uncle Roy turned around and walked back to my bedside. "I was exasperated with myself and with my men," he said, "but I should have thanked you that morning. I'd like to thank you now." And then he smiled at me. "Will you please forgive me?" He stretched his hand out and I reached back to him and shook it, and then I smiled.

"Of course, I forgive you, Uncle Roy," I said, as my cheeks grew red and tears began to fill my eyes. "You're my favorite cop in the world!"

Uncle Roy laughed. "I really *am* proud of you," he said, "proud of all three of you." He then glanced over at my sister. "I'm not absolutely certain that Angela would be here today if it hadn't of been for you."

I looked over at my sister, who was sleeping soundly. I felt the tears roll down my cheeks. I wasn't even embarrassed by them anymore. I didn't seem to have any control over them. Anyway, they were good tears – tears of joy and relief. We had done it, Lizzie, Scottie, and I. We had solved the mystery and found my sister. I had never been happier in my entire life.

☙ 38 ❧

After my father received his degree from the University of Washington, he moved our family out of Seattle back to Richland. Lizzie and I were together again. When the time came, she and I decided to go to Seattle to college. Interestingly, Scottie decided to go to college there as well.

In the end, neither Lizzie nor Scottie nor I actually became sleuths. Lizzie studied psychology and was working on her master's degree in social work at the University of Washington. Scottie was at Seattle University's School of Law. And I, well, I decided that I wanted to become a writer. Maybe it was all those notes that I was always taking as a kid. After getting my undergraduate degree, I ended up going to the other side of the country, to New Orleans, where Faulkner had written his first novel.

☙ ❧

It was Thanksgiving weekend, fifteen years later, and the entire Johnson family had gathered in Seattle, since most of the family lived there. On Saturday, Angela and I decided to meet at Pike Place Market for lunch. I had lost track of time while wandering through the market, and I arrived at Café Sport a few minutes late. Angela was already seated at a table near the window, and she was looking over the menu. On the wall behind her was a blackboard with the day's specials written in chalk.

"Oh, good, they have Chum," I said, as I hung my purse off the back of my chair and sat down. "That's exactly what I'm in the mood for." Angela smiled and nodded.

"Yum, that sounds good," she said, closing her menu. I looked at my sister. Except for her tired eyes, she still looked like a teenager.

"This is nice, Angela," I said. "We never got a chance to be alone yesterday."

Angela laughed. "I rarely get to be alone, period," she said, rolling her eyes.

I nodded. "Your kids are so adorable, Angela," I said. "You know that if I lived here, I would love to babysit anytime." Angela had two daughters who were five and three. I could not have loved them more if they had been my own.

"Well, maybe some day," she said. "You know we would love that!" Angela had gotten married after her second year of college. It sounded trite to say, but they had been too young. Money was a huge issue, and then there was the cute little blonde at his office.

The marriage had come to an early end. Angela had been devastated when Joseph left her, of course, but she was really brave about it. She took the girls and moved back in with our parents and, with their help, finished the final two years of her undergraduate work. She earned a degree in education and was doing substitute work at the local elementary school. She planned on eventually becoming a third-grade teacher. Considering everything, she had weathered the storms of the last few years really well.

I was still single, and I wasn't exactly sure where I wanted to live after I finished grad school, but I loved the idea of being close to my family.

The waiter came, carrying a basket of rolls, still steaming from the oven. We both ordered the salmon, and then we dove into the bread and butter.

"You know who I was thinking of the other day?" I asked Angela in between bites.

"Who?" she asked, as she reached for her water glass.

"Tom Walters," I said casually. "What ever happened to him?"

"Wow – Tom Walters," Angela said placing her glass back down. "I don't know where he's at right now, but I do know that he got in to med school."

"Oh, did he really? I remember him being torn between going into medicine and becoming a pro-baseball player," I said, taking a bite of bread.

Angela laughed. "Yeah, that's right, back when he was seventeen. But I heard that he eventually chose medicine."

"Good for him. He was an amazing guy. I'm sure you knew that I had a serious crush on him back then?"

"Bobbi, you were like ten, weren't you?"

"Yeah, but a girl can dream, can't she?" I laughed. "I think I fell in love with him when he complimented me on my boy haircut. You remember how Mom got in that phase of keeping my hair so short?"

"Yes, I do," Angela said and she laughed. "She called it a Pixie cut, right?"

I nodded my head. "Ugh. Don't ever do that to your daughters, you promise?" Angela laughingly vowed never to be so cruel.

"So, whatever happened to you and Tom? I mean, you don't have to talk about this if you don't want to, but back then I never had the nerve to ask you."

"Oh, no, it's okay. It was so long ago." I noticed that Angela had stopped eating at the first mention of Tom's name. "You know, to be honest with you, I really don't know what happened."

"You're kidding. You guys never got back together after – well, after you got back home?"

"No, we didn't. He visited me at the hospital once, and I expected him to come over after I finally got out, but he didn't."

"Didn't he ever call you?" I asked. I was seriously surprised because I remembered how much he had liked Angela. I remembered his passionate love letters, and I remembered that he was such a nice guy. It didn't seem logical that he would have just dropped out of the picture.

Angela was shaking her head. "No, he didn't. He never tried to get in touch with me again."

"Did you ever try to call him?" I asked her, as I began to butter another slice of bread. Angela still hadn't touched her bread and I figured someone had to eat it.

"Yeah, I did. I called him and talked with his younger brother. He was nice. I called him and left messages with his parents. I tried to get his attention at church, but he pretended not to see me." I watched Angela's face and, if I wasn't mistaken, she was blushing. "I finally reached him by telephone one day and I kind of made a fool of myself I think."

"What do you mean?" I asked her. "What did you say?"

"Nothing, really. I didn't say anything but 'hi' and then he just started to yell at me."

"He yelled at you? What did he say?" I suddenly lost all interest in my bread.

"All he said was that I should never call him again. I was just kind of blabbering, 'but I don't understand' or something stupid and he said, 'Have I made myself clear enough?' I didn't know what to say, and in the end, I didn't say anything because he hung up on me."

"Tom Walters hung up on you? What in the world? I mean – I can hardly believe that. I know that he really liked you." I had never told Angela that I had read all of the love notes that I had found under her bed. Somehow, I wanted to tell her that I knew about them, but I decided to hold my tongue. Angela shrugged.

"I thought that he did, too. In fact, do you know what he used to say about us before, you know, the whole incident?" I shook my head. "He used to say that we were soul mates," Angela said, with a little smile on her face.

"Really? He was a romantic at seventeen years old? I'm twenty-five and I still haven't met a true romantic."

"I know. There aren't very many men who know how to express their feelings. But Tom could. He had a way with words. And the thing is, he was right, Bobbi, we were soul mates. It was amazing!" she said. "No matter what we'd be discussing, we would find out that we felt exactly the same way about it. Whether it was about something as serious as our faith, or as simple as a song on the radio, when he would begin to talk about something, he would get real passionate about it. He was always so enthusiastic, you know? And I would be listening to him and would be thinking, 'Me too, me too!'" Angela's cheeks grew unmistakably pink, and she quickly reached for a sesame-seed encrusted breadstick and started to break it into little pieces.

"I remember, Angela," I said, nodding my head. "I honestly do. You two were so cute together." I really had noticed these things about Tom and Angela, even when I was a kid, and I hadn't been joking with Angela when I'd told her that I had had a serious crush on Tom Walters. I think that I was maybe even a little jealous of her back then.

As I sat there thinking about what Angela said about how she'd felt about Tom, I realized why I was still single. I had witnessed the chemistry – or whatever you wanted to call it – between Angela and Tom, and that was what I had been waiting for. It's not that I hadn't met a lot of guys. I had, and they were all nice, and a lot of them had really wanted to get serious with me, but I was waiting to feel about someone the way Angela had felt about Tom. It kind of made my heart hurt, even fifteen years later. I wasn't sure that I was ever going to be able to experience that kind of love, and I would rather remain single than settle for something less. I didn't want ordinary. I wanted extraordinary.

"Well, I am so sorry that he hurt you like that, Angela. I always thought that you had broken up with him for some reason. I had no idea that he betrayed you!"

"Oh, no, he didn't betray me! He must've had a good reason." Angela sighed and shook her head. "If I tell you something, do you promise that you will keep it between you and me?"

I nodded very seriously, and she continued. "I had completely fallen in love with him, and I mean, completely. I know that I was young, but he was my first true love," she said. "He was my first true love, and he was my first broken heart. Actually, Bobbi, he was my *only* broken heart."

"Before Joseph, you mean?"

Angela looked at me and shook her head. "I know that sounds terrible, and I'm not saying that I didn't love Joseph, Bobbi, because I did. But, there had been a lot of hurtful things said and done before he left me, so when he finally did leave, I was almost relieved," Angela said. "With Tom, there had been nothing but sweetness and pleasure. He made me feel so smart and so funny and so beautiful. When I lost him, I felt like I had lost the best part of me too." By this time Angela had completely shredded her breadstick and she reached for another one.

I didn't know what to say, so, probably for the first time in my life, I didn't say anything. Suddenly, Angela looked straight into my eyes.

"You know what the truth is?" This time I shook my head. "Every once in a while, I still think about him," Angela said, "and I still wonder what it is that I did wrong."

"What *you* did wrong?" I said incredulously, and then I covered my mouth as a few of the other diners looked over at me from nearby tables. "Angela, what you did wrong?" I repeated in a hushed voice across the table. "He's the one who messed up.

How could he have gone from declaring his love for you one minute to totally denying it the next?" Angela didn't say anything. She was looking out at the street, seeing right through the many pedestrians who were walking past us.

"Ugh!" she said softly. "Who knew that this could still hurt so much?" She gave me a weak little smile. "I have made it a practice not to think of Tom Walters, Bobbi."

"Oh, Angela," I cried, "I am so sorry."

"No, I didn't mean to make you feel bad," she said. "I hate to admit it, but, in spite of my good intentions, I think about him all the time, and every time I think about him, I feel sad. I feel sad, and I cringe with embarrassment," she said, shaking her head. "I don't know, I couldn't make any sense out of it back then and I can't make any sense out of it now."

"Who could make sense of it?" I said. "I mean, you knew the way that he truly felt about you, and then it just appeared like he stopped feeling that way. It really doesn't add up, so you figured it must have been something you did."

Angela nodded her head in agreement. She looked so young and vulnerable. "Oh, Angela – you've been carrying this pain around for such a long time." She shrugged her shoulders and then picked up her glass and took a sip of water.

"You know, Bobbi, I've never told another soul about this," she said, letting out a little laugh. "And I am so sorry that you're the lucky one that I'm dumping it on now."

"Are you kidding? No, I'm glad that you are sharing all of this with me. I really had no idea," I said.

Angela took a deep breath. "Yeah, I know. I've purposely kept it all to myself. Everybody has spent so much energy worrying about me, I really didn't want to add anything else for you to worry about. The truth is, though, that it was harder for me to get over Tom than it was for me to get over, you know, the whole horrible thing that happened to me back then."

"That breaks my heart, Angela," I said. "I wish that I could have been there for you." I reached over and squeezed her hand, and then I got an idea. "You know what I think you should do?" I said. "I think you should try to get in touch with him now, and ask him what in the world was going on in his head back then."

"Oh, yeah, right. 'Hi Tom, it's me, Angela, from a hundred years ago? I was wondering, why did you break my heart back then?'"

I laughed. "Yeah, something like that."

"You're crazy. Never in a million years," she said. "For one thing, he's a big time doctor now, off saving the world."

"And you got your teaching degree, you are the best mother ever, and you are still the nicest girl in the whole wide world! He should be so lucky to hear from you," I declared. I just wished that Angela could realize how incredible she was.

"There is no way, Bobbi. I would be too scared," Angela said.

"Scared? Why would you be scared to get in touch with him?" I asked her. Angela looked at the tiny breadcrumb mountain that she had made on the tablecloth and laughed.

"If you can believe this, I would be scared that he would still think that I was chasing after him. I'm sure that's why he got so mad on the phone back then. Nothing is worse than an aggressive woman."

"Chasing after him? Oh, come on Angela. First of all, calling him back then was only normal. You were just trying to find out what was going on! That wasn't aggressive behavior. And second, by this time he's probably married, don't you think? It wouldn't be about getting back together with him," I said. "It would be about getting closure. Don't you think that it would be good to resolve this thing?"

"You know, I do think," she admitted. "I've always wanted to know what really happened, and I've actually always wanted to tell him how proud I was of him for getting into med school. But, I don't know, it's just not going to happen."

"Why not?" I asked. Sometimes I still worried about Angela. She had had so much taken away from her fifteen years ago, and then again, more recently. I just wanted everything in her life to be perfect now, or at least for her to have a little peace in her heart. She was looking across the table at me with a very serious expression on her face.

"Because, Bobbi," she said, "I would just be too scared." I shook my head like I didn't understand and was going to speak, but Angela continued. "I would be too scared that he would somehow hurt me, and I don't ever want to go through that kind of pain again." Angela looked away from me, and this time there were tears in her eyes.

"Oh, Angela," I said, taking her hand into mine. "I'm so sorry that I brought this up! The last thing that I wanted to do was to make you sad!" Angela waved her napkin at me like it was nothing, like she was just being silly, and that she was sorry. But I still felt awful and I wanted to redeem the conversation. "Angela, he would never hurt you again. He was so young. He probably feels terrible about the way he treated you. He probably would be relieved to tell you how sorry he was and is. You know that he still feels guilty to this day," I said. Angela looked at me and rolled her eyes."

"Yeah, right. It's probably keeping him up at nights."

I smiled at her. "Probably," I agreed. "Anyway, what do I know? But, I just think that it would be nice for you to get a message from him telling you what he's been up to, and also telling you that he realizes what an idiot he was, and that he is more sorry than he can say et cetera, et cetera, et cetera..." I laughed, but Angela just shook her head like she didn't see it happening.

"Okay, okay," I said, "forget that I brought it up." I looked at Angela. She had a wistful look on her face, and it made me feel bad. It made me want to call Tom up myself and tell him that he owed Angela a big apology! I hated that he had hurt her like this, and I wanted to fix it.

"Bobbi, don't get that look," Angela said. "This is not a mystery that you have to solve!" I laughed at that, and she continued. "It's really no big deal. I mean, it's not that I wouldn't like to find out what was going on in his head back then, believe me! But, in the end, it doesn't really matter."

I sighed. Relationships confused me. I personally felt like anything could be resolved by talking it through. I was big into friendship, and not just between the same sexes. I believed in true platonic friendship. I mean, in the scheme of things, what is more important on this earth than real, true-blue friends? But maybe I was just naïve.

"Hey, You Guys. There you are!" Angela and I looked over at the voice that was calling out to us. Speaking of true-blue friends...

"Hey," I said, "I was just thinking about you two." It was Lizzie and Scottie, coming to join us for dessert. Angela and I got up and hugged them and then moved over so they could fit at our table.

"I wasn't sure that you were actually going to be able to join us. I'm so glad you did," Angela said, and I think I detected a bit of relief in her voice. But she quickly looked my way and smiled at me.

Over a rush of apologies and explanations, Scottie and Lizzie set all their stuff down and gave their order to the waiter. They then went to the restrooms to wash their hands. Angela reached over, took my hand, and squeezed it for a moment.

"It was good to talk to you about this, Bobbi. I don't let myself think about some things, you know? Probably as a protection measure or something. But I'm glad that I got to tell you about Tom. He was a beautiful part of my life, and, well, I wish that I was like you. If I was, I would probably..."

"I'm back," Lizzie said, and she slid into her chair. Angela didn't finish her thought. Instead, she and I both turned our attention to Lizzie.

I had gotten my childhood dream. Lizzie and I were sisters now. She and Scottie had gotten married that spring, and even as they were exchanging their vows, I was sure that their marriage had been ordained from the beginning of time. It was a dream come true for me and, judging from the way they mooned over each other, I was pretty sure that it was a dream come true for them too. Happily ever after had never been a more fitting description of the union of a boy and a girl.

I guess that I have always had dreams, but I would never have considered myself to be a dreamer. No, early on in the process of growing up, I had become a realist. I looked back at Angela, who was now chatting happily with Lizzie and Scottie. I was quite certain that Angela had become a realist, too.

It wasn't that Angela and I had given up all of our dreams. I knew that I, most definitely, was still very hopeful about the future. I wondered about Angela. Would she dare to dream again? I hoped that she would. I hoped that I hadn't been wrong to bring up the past. I would definitely have to give her a call next week and make sure she knew that I hadn't meant to upset her. But, to be honest, isn't that what family is for? We stick our noses into each other's business and then try to rectify everything afterwards. But, at least we really care about each other. What would life be like if we didn't have people in our lives who cared enough about us to bring up real issues?

I was pretty sure that Angela realized that I only wanted her to be happy. I wanted for any and every painful issue in her life to be resolved. I was so lucky to have her in my life. No matter what I went through, she was always there to encourage me – just like when I was a kid.

If you had asked me at the age of ten to describe myself, I would have told you that I was an optimist. I believed that if a person was selfless; if she was full of dreams that only God could place in her heart and soul – that she would be able to accomplish great things – things that would prevail beyond her own lifetime. I believed that then and, even after fifteen years, I believed it still. I looked around the table at the sweet faces of my lifelong friends. Truly, how could I be anything but a believer?

❧ Epilogue ❧

Dear Angela,

I'm sure that you were shocked to see the return address. Yes, it's me, Tom Walters. I got a call the other day from your sister, Bobbi. It was great to hear from her. We figured out, it's been around fifteen years. I can hardly believe it. I hope you don't mind, but I asked Bobbi for your address. I've been wanting to write to you for a long time, but never could work up the nerve. I've kept up with news about you through your old friend, Theresa. She's a physical therapist at the hospital where I work.

Yes, I finally became a doctor. You remember that I had dreamed of becoming one back when we were in high school? I gave up on the baseball idea in college – kind of a humbling experience…

I heard that you had married, but are now single with two children. I'm sorry, I'm sure that these last few years have not been easy ones for you. With school and residency and work and all, I have just never found the time to get married.

I just re-read that last sentence – and, I have to admit, it was pretty lame. Obviously, it's not only about the time.

I would like to talk with you, Angela. I understand if you are not interested in speaking with me. I was a real jerk. I cannot tell you how badly I have felt about the way I treated you fifteen years ago. There is no excuse for the way I acted. If I was you, I would never want to talk to me again, and I don't blame you if that's the way you still feel. I'm going to tell you why I think I acted the way I did, but I want you to know that I'm not trying to make excuses.

You were taken from me by a madman. I was seventeen and so in love with you that it hurt. I acted really stoic back then because I was afraid that if I let myself feel, I would completely lose it. I didn't talk to anybody about what I was going through the whole time that you were missing and afterwards. The relief that I felt after I heard that they found you alive was so intense that I literally had to hide myself in my closet and weep. It scared me. I felt so weak, so vulnerable.

I went to see you at the hospital and you looked like a little girl. I think they told me that you weighed around seventy five pounds at that point. I was so angry that I was shaking. I didn't want your parents to see me that way, so I left.

Angela, the overwhelming emotions that I felt at that time confused me so much. On the one hand, I wanted to take you in my arms and pretend like everything was just like it had been before. On the other hand, I wanted to find that guy and pummel him to death with my fists. I wanted to torture him like he had tortured you, and then I wanted to kill him. I'm being honest with you. I wanted to kill him.

That was hard for me to reconcile. How could I even think about becoming a doctor, a person whose sole purpose is to save lives, and at the same time want to murder someone with my own hands? It was too hard for me to figure out, so, and I am so ashamed of this, Angela, I decided that it would be easier to put it all out of my mind and to go on with my life. And that's what I did. I purposely stopped thinking about you and about what happened to you, and about how I felt about you, and I concentrated on my studies and on baseball. And now here I am, fifteen years later, successful, I guess, but alone.

Don't get me wrong, I have dated and invested time in a lot of women over the years. I have truly wanted to meet the woman of my dreams, but, at the end of the day, none of these women even came close to you, Angela. The way that I felt about any of these women just didn't compare to the way that I had felt about you.

You are probably thinking, then why didn't you give me a call? And you're right. I should have given you a call, but at first I'd heard that you'd gotten married, and then, even after I'd heard that you had gotten a divorce, I felt like you were out of my reach. Why would you be interested in me when I had been such a jerk?

I've got to tell you, when I heard Bobbi's voice on the phone, I thought that it was you at first, and – well, let's just say that I was really happy to hear your voice. Fifteen years, Angela, and just the thought of you...

Okay, anyway. I wanted to let you know that I am here. I hope that you will forgive me for betraying you when you most needed me. I have carried around a sense of grief for these many, many years. I am truly sorry. I would like to think that I have done some serious maturing since then.

Can I call you? Please let me know.

I hope the answer is yes.

$-$ Tom

❧ The End ❧